'You're serious? You honestly don't want to get married?'

'Correct.'

'You would make such a wonderful father, Hayden. Look at the way you bandaged my knee this morning.'

'I'm a doctor, Annie.'

'You'd be wonderful with children,' she said softly.

Hayden felt a twisting in his gut and wondered how things had escalated so fast. It was Annie. Never before had a woman got beneath his skin so quickly.

'I know, my daughter Liana died when she was four weeks old.'

'Oh, Hayden,' she whispered.

'Out of my mockery of a marriage came the most precious gift and then that, too, was taken away from me.' He shook his head and unlocked his door.

She wanted to go to him, to comfort him. She felt closer to him right this very second than she had to any other man in her life.

Lucy Clark began writing romance in her early teens and immediately knew she'd found her 'calling' in life. After working as a secretary in a busy teaching hospital, she turned her hand to writing medical romance. She currently lives in South Australia with her husband and two children. Lucy largely credits her writing success to the support of her husband, family and friends.

Recent titles by the same author:

ENGLISHMAN AT DINGO CREEK
EMERGENCY: DECEPTION
THE DOCTOR'S GIFT
THE OUTBACK DOCTOR

THE REGISTRAR'S WEDDING WISH

BY
LUCY CLARK

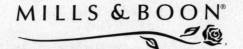

MILLS & BOON®

To Rachael – thanks for the support & the laughter
Prov 15:16

*All the characters in this book have no existence outside the imagination
of the author, and have no relation whatsoever to anyone bearing the
same name or names. They are not even distantly inspired by any
individual known or unknown to the author, and all the incidents are
pure invention.*

*First published in Great Britain 2003
Harlequin Mills & Boon Limited,
Eton House, 18-24 Paradise Road, Richmond, Surrey TW9 1SR*

© Lucy Clark 2003

ISBN 0 263 83874 9

*Set in Times Roman 10½ on 11 pt.
03-0104-53822*

*Printed and bound in Spain
by Litografía Rosés, S.A., Barcelona*

CHAPTER ONE

'I DON'T want to sound like a cliché, Annie, but give it more time.'

Annie wrinkled her nose at her friend's advice. 'Time-shmime. What I need is a change.'

'A *change*? Annie! Your apartment burnt down, you split up with Adam and cancelled your wedding, your dad's company is in financial difficulty and now you've moved into a new apartment. Isn't that *enough* change?' Natasha asked incredulously.

She sighed. 'It wasn't the kind of change I was hoping for.'

'I know,' Natasha soothed. 'How are you going with the boxes? Finished sorting them out yet?'

Annie looked around her new apartment and sighed into the telephone receiver. 'No.'

'Want me to come and help? Brenton's just arrived home from the hospital so he can supervise the children with their homework tonight.'

'It's a tempting offer but I think I'll just wade through things slowly.' She opened a box and peered inside. Ribbons and trophies from her childhood were packed haphazardly with nursing reference books and kitchen utensils. 'Besides, both you and Monty—' she used the high school nickname for Natasha's husband '—have gone above and beyond the call of friendship during the past few months.'

'OK, but you call me if you need anything.'

'I will.' Annie rang off and replaced the receiver. Sighing again, she opened another box which contained more medical books and reached inside. 'Ugh, this is a heavy one,' she muttered, using both hands to lift the reference book out. She felt something soft brush the edge of her fingers and, looking down, saw an enormous brown huntsman spider about to crawl onto her hand.

'Aagh!' She screamed and catapulted the book across the room where it landed with a heavy thud between two more boxes. 'Eww, eww, eww.' Her skin was creeping and crawling and when she saw the spider climb the side of another box to hide inside, she shivered uncomfortably.

Hopping over boxes and miscellaneous items that were lying around, she headed for the door. 'Eww, eww, eww.' As she wrenched down on the doorhandle, she accidentally bent her thumb backwards. 'Ow, ow, ow. Oh this isn't happening, this isn't happening,' she muttered as she cradled her hand against her. Whimpering, she knocked on the door of the next apartment, hoping the person who lived there was braver than she was when it came to spiders.

Looking down at her thumb while she waited, she gently checked the range of motion. 'Ow,' she whimpered again. The door opened and she looked up into a pair of the bluest eyes she'd ever seen.

'Can I help you?' The man's voice was gruff and impatient.

Annie's mind went blank and her jaw sagged open as she shifted her gaze away from his eyes to briefly encompass the rest of him. He was dressed in a pair of blue surfing board-shorts, his brown chest bare.

'Er…' she started, and then cleared her throat. Come on brain—work! 'Um…I'm Annie…from next door.' She gestured to her apartment and then whimpered again as she remembered her thumb.

'Have you hurt your hand?'

'Oh, no. It's OK. Just bent my thumb back.'

Without warning, he reached for her hand and peered closely at the digit in question. Annie was surprised at the contact from this handsome stranger, his touch warm and tender as he moved the thumb slightly around. 'Doesn't seem broken.' He let it go as abruptly as he'd taken it. 'Was there anything else? I was just about to take a shower.'

'Oh!' The image of this man standing beneath the cooling spray of a shower did nothing to help her present state of tonguetiedness. 'Uh…well, I won't keep you…'

'Fine.' He started to close his door.

'But I have a spider in my apartment,' she rushed on. 'And I was kind of wondering if you wouldn't mind…' She shrugged. 'You know, getting it out…for me…please?' She raised her eyebrows hopefully.

He took a set of keys off the wall before closing his door and stalking into her apartment. 'Where is it?'

'Well…' Anne could feel the creeping, crawling sensation return. 'It was on my book but after I threw it across the room—'

'The spider?'

'Eww. Yuck. I threw the book *with* the spider on…it.' She screwed up her nose as she pointed to where the textbook lay, the hard cover making a steeple on the ground, the white pages in the middle now slightly crumpled.

He walked over and picked up the book, making sure the pages were straight. 'So that's what that noise was. Sounded as though you were dropping bricks. Medical and surgical nursing, eh?' He placed the book on top of an unopened box. 'Where did the spider go after you'd hurled it—and your book—across the room?'

'It…' Annie shivered again '…crawled up that box.' She pointed, keeping well away. Her dark-haired saviour opened the flap on the box.

'Ah, there he is. Probably more scared of you—'

'Than I am of him. Yeah, yeah, I know. I don't have anything against him—'

'Except that you want him out of your apartment?'

'Exactly.'

He straightened and looked around the room. He picked up a piece of paper before walking into the kitchen and coming back with a glass. Annie grimaced, vowing to throw the glass out as soon as he'd finished.

'Open the door to the stairwell.'

Annie rushed to do as he ordered, glad she didn't have to watch him catch the wretched thing. Moments later, he came out of her apartment and she shuddered as he walked past with the spider trapped between the paper and the glass. 'Eww, eww, eww, eww, eww,' she muttered, closing her eyes.

'Go in front of me and open the outside door,' he instructed. Annie opened her eyes and raced down the stairs as though her life depended on it. She opened the door, looking the other way as he passed her again and took the spider to the row of native trees which grew between their apartment building and the house next door.

She couldn't bear to look. 'Here you go,' he said, holding the paper and glass, minus its occupant, out to her. Annie grimaced and shook her head. 'Throw them away?' he asked and at her nod he deposited them in one of the bins.

'You probably should have recycled that glass but…I do understand.'

'You do?' She was surprised. They walked back up the stairs to their apartments, Annie sneaking glances at the defined muscles of his back.

'I have three sisters and all of them react to spiders the way you do.'

Annie laughed. 'My hero.' Outside her apartment door she held out her hand to her neighbour. 'Thanks again. I really do appreciate it.' When he simply smiled but didn't shake her hand, she frowned a little.

'I don't want to hurt your thumb.'

Annie looked down at the digit in question. 'Oh, yeah. I'd forgotten.'

'It's obviously not hurting any more.'

'Just aching…a little.' She smiled shyly, unable to believe she was standing here with a relative stranger discussing her thumb. 'Should be fine.'

'I take it that you're trained in the medical profession? Either that or you use heavy nursing texts instead of dumb-bells.' His words were dry but she noted the twinkle of teasing in his eyes.

'Or maybe I use them for hurling spiders across the room.' That got a smile from him—small though it was. Annie started to feel even more self-conscious, standing in the middle of the hallway. His shoulders were so…broad and when he smiled like that, her stomach did flips and her knees went weak. 'Would you like to come in for a cool drink?' The second she offered, she remembered the only thing cool she had to drink was tap water. 'No.' She tapped her forehead with her hand. 'Sorry. I've just remembered I don't *have* anything cool to drink.'

He peered around her open door. 'You don't have any furniture either. Planning to sleep in one of those boxes tonight?'

'Hmm.' She gave him a thoughtful look. 'Now, there's an idea. I was wondering what I was going to do.' He raised an eyebrow at her words and she laughed. 'I have a futon in the bedroom. My apartment burnt down a few months ago,' she added by way of explanation.

'But you managed to save your belongings?' He gestured to the mound of boxes.

'I'd…um…already packed them up and moved them… elsewhere when the fire happened.' Annie looked down at the ground, trying to control her thoughts. Now was no time to be thinking about the past.

'That was fortunate.'

'Yeah.' She bit her lower lip, hoping her emotions wouldn't overpower her.

'Was it a painful break-up?' His insightful question was asked quietly and Annie brought her gaze back to his. How did he know? Unless…

'Been there yourself?' she enquired just as boldly.

He forced a smile. 'Let's not go there.'

'My sentiments exactly. Well…thank you for rescuing me.'

'My pleasure. Let me know when you find the other one.'

'Other what?'

'The other huntsman.'

'*What?*'

'Huntsmen always have a mate. Ever since the Ark—they travel in twos.'

'Ewww.' She squirmed again. 'You mean there's *another* one in my apartment!'

Her neighbour laughed at her expression and for a moment, she took comfort in that deep, rich sound. 'Relax. He'll be more frightened of you—'

'Yeah, yeah.' Annie impatiently waved his words away and frowned at the stack of boxes waiting to be unpacked, feeling quite ill. 'I wonder if I can just throw all that out and buy new stuff,' she mumbled thoughtfully.

Another rich chuckle emanated from the man beside her and she realised she really liked the sound. Her gaze flicked to his chest before quickly meeting his eyes again. 'No need to go *that* far. Why don't you leave the unpacking until you get more furniture?'

'Can't. The furniture is being delivered tomorrow, which is why I need to sort a lot of this stuff out tonight.' She sighed heavily.

'What time is it being delivered?'

'Who knows? They said morning, which could mean anything.' She shrugged. 'I won't be here anyway.'

'I suppose you want me to keep a lookout for them?'

'No. No. Not at all. A friend of mine has the morning off so she's offered to come over.' Annie shrugged, feeling a little self-conscious about telling this half-naked stranger more about her life than he probably wanted to know. 'My shift got changed at the last minute.'

'Nurse?'

'No. I used to be.'

He nodded. 'That explains the textbooks.'

'I'm a doctor now.'

'A doctor,' he repeated, his dark eyebrows raised in surprise. 'I suppose you work at Geelong General hospital.'

'Yes.' Annie lifted her chin and straightened her shoulders. Was there something wrong with what she did for a living? Adam had initially been intrigued by her job but then he'd come to resent it.

Hayden liked the way her dark eyes flashed with defiance and felt an unwanted twisting in his gut. Had someone dared to criticise her career choice in the past?

Annie thought back to the way her neighbour had tenderly examined her hand and she narrowed her gaze. 'Why?' She asked slowly. 'Do *you* work there?'

'I start on Monday.'

Annie's jaw dropped open slightly before she grabbed hold of her senses and forced her mind to work in an orderly and rational manner. Even before she asked the question, she instinctively knew the answer. 'Orthopaedics?' She held her breath.

'Yes.'

Her mouth went dry. There was only one person starting in the orthopaedic department on Monday and that was her new boss—Professor Hayden Robinson.

'Do I presume by the pained look on your face that *you* work in Orthopaedics?'

Annie smiled at his words. 'It's not *pained*…just… amazed. I mean, what are the odds?'

'True.'

They both stood, staring at each other. The moment stretched into an uncomfortable silence. Annie's stomach churned with uncontrollable butterflies as she continued to gaze into those hypnotic blue eyes. Her brain refused to function properly and although she knew she should say something to snap them out of it, she couldn't for the life of her think what.

'I need to go.' He stepped back and put the key into the lock.

'Yeah.' She cleared her throat and took a step in the opposite direction.

He unlocked his door and pushed it open. 'See you on Monday, *neighbour*.' His smile was one that went directly to her heart, piercing it with giddy schoolgirl laughter.

Annie choked the laugh down and forced a polite smile. She knew she should move but couldn't. She watched him move into his apartment and close the door. The smile faded and it took another half a minute before she could force her legs to work.

Her new boss was her new neighbour!

She went back into her apartment and checked the time. It was only seven o'clock so she picked up the phone and dialled Natasha's number.

'You'll never guess who my neighbour is,' she said into the receiver a few seconds later. She told her friend about the close encounter with the spider and how her neighbour had come to her rescue. She also learnt that Brenton had found a huntsman spider when they'd been transferring the boxes to the new apartment.

'So chances are you found the mate this evening.'

Annie felt a little disappointed that she wouldn't be calling on her sexy neighbour to help her out.

'Anyway,' Natasha continued, 'what's he like?'

'Tall, dark and very handsome,' Annie said with a laugh. 'Oh, but I made him throw the glass out. I'm sorry, Natasha—I'll buy you and Monty a new set to replace the ones I borrowed, but I just couldn't keep it. The thought of washing it…eww.' She shuddered.

'Who cares about the glass?' Natasha replied. 'Tell me more about Professor Robinson.'

Annie sat cross-legged on the floor and leaned back against the wall. 'He has broad shoulders and a nice chest.'

'You saw his chest!'

'He was naked—from the waist up,' she added quickly.

'Why? What had he been doing?'

'How should I know? All he was wearing were board-shorts and a light sprinkling of sand. Swimming? Running on the beach? How should I know?' she repeated.

'Did you count the grains of sand?'

'No! Stop teasing.'

'Why? He sounds like just what you need.'

'I do not need another failed relationship. I've had enough of those to last me a lifetime. Besides, his tastes probably run to the gorgeous supermodel type.'

'You don't know that.'

'Yeah, well, most men like that.'

'Brenton doesn't.'

'Have you looked in the mirror lately, Tash? You *are* the gorgeous supermodel type. I'm not.'

'Stop it. Stop it right now,' Natasha demanded. 'I tell you, all the guys you've dated in the past have done an excellent job in destroying your self-esteem. You're a beautiful, intelligent woman, Annie, and I'm not just saying that because I'm your friend. Have *you* looked in the mirror lately?'

'Yes.'

'And what do you see?'

'A woman with boring, uneven brown eyes, a crooked nose, a mouth that's too big and ears that look pointed if my boring brown, out-of-control, short, curly hair doesn't cover them. And to top it all off, I'm not exactly tall.'

'You're five foot four, Annie. That's not short.'

'Feels it.'

'If that's really how you see yourself, then you're look-ing in the wrong mirror, my friend, because I see someone completely different. Your face has character and I love the story about how you broke your nose.'

'Character. Right. That's just another way of saying I'm ugly.'

'You are not and I don't want to hear you talking like that. Annie…you're beautiful.'

'Yeah?'

'Yeah. I'd give anything to have your natural curls and so would a lot of other women. You are generous, nurturing and clever.'

'So why don't the men I date stick around?'

'Maybe they're intimidated by your brilliance?'

'Yeah, right.' Annie laughed but it ended on a sigh. 'I'm going to be forty soon, Tash. *Forty!* I just want to get married, have children and be happy.'

'And you will.'

'When?'

'I don't know but give it some time. It's only been three months since you called off the wedding.'

'Since *Adam* called off the wedding, you mean.'

'You told me it was a mutual agreement.'

'Yeah…but he voiced the idea first.'

'But you were thinking it, you even told me as much. Anyway, I'm not suggesting you get serious with Mr Gorgeous-Next-Door—'

'*Professor* Gorgeous-Next-Door to you.' Annie tried to inject a bit of humour into the conversation.

'Whatever… But…I don't know, use him as a mental diversion.'

'A mental diversion? Are you listening to yourself?'

'Must be Brenton's bad influence.' Natasha laughed. 'Look. Every woman needs a transitional man and I just—'

'Are you crazy? In three days' time, he'll be my boss!'

'As women, we focus our minds on problems far too conscientiously. We get so wrapped up in things, nuances, gestures, innuendoes. You were the one wanting a change—all I'm suggesting here is a change in mental thought. You don't need to follow through with anything, just allow yourself some private little…I don't know…'

'Fantasies?' Annie supplied.

'Flirtations,' Natasha said firmly. 'Sometimes, just the *idea* that someone else might be interested in you can go a long way to restoring self-confidence. Do you follow? It might help to just lighten your thoughts and that way you might start sleeping a bit better at night.'

'How did you—'

'You lived in our house after the fire, Annie. Even though you were doing shifts, I know the signs of a restless sleeper. I used to be one years ago, remember?'

'Yeah.'

'Think about it,' Natasha ventured. 'I have to go. It's time for Rachael and the twins to go to bed so I'd better go kiss them goodnight.'

'Give them one from me.'

'Will do. Speak to you tomorrow. Bye.'

After Annie had replaced the receiver, she stayed on the floor, thinking over what Natasha had said and finally decided her friend had a point. Perhaps what she needed was a little mental diversion. It wouldn't be anything serious and it certainly wouldn't *mean* anything.

The sound of water running came through the walls and she remembered her neighbour saying he was about to have a shower.

Her neighbour!

Professor Hayden Robinson!

She rested her head against the wall and closed her eyes, focusing on the sound of the shower. The water cascading down over his crop of dark hair, plastering it to his head. The way he would lift his arms to wash the sand and salt from his hair, his blue eyes hidden beneath his eyelids. The soapy bubbles, sliding down his neck, over his broad shoulders, across his rigid abdomen and down towards—

'Whoa!' Annie sat forward and opened her eyes. 'Whoa, girl!' She realised her heart rate had increased and that her mouth was dry. Why had she listened to Natasha?

She rose from the floor and stalked into the kitchen, stepping firmly over the boxes and obstacles in her way. Reaching for one of the five remaining glasses she'd borrowed, she shoved it beneath the tap and filled it with water.

'You do *not* need to fill your head with silly and childish schoolgirl fantasies—especially about your boss!' she scolded herself before drinking the water. 'You have an early morning so finish getting organised and get to bed.'

With a firm nod she did just that, wishing she'd borrowed the radio Natasha had offered. Instead, she sang some of her favourite songs as she went through each box…very carefully, sorting them out into categories which would make it easier once the furniture arrived.

As she lay down on her futon almost three hours later, Annie felt pleased. She hadn't found another spider so felt more comfortable about going to sleep. She'd accomplished a lot and tomorrow she had yet another busy shift ahead of her, but as she closed her eyes and started to drift off to sleep, she couldn't stop the images of her tall, dark professor from entering her dreams.

Annie had been on duty for three hours and it felt like for ever. She'd done a ward round, set two fractured arms, organised surgery for a patient with a fractured femur and now her pager was beeping again. Just as well it wasn't a clinic day or she'd be *completely* frazzled.

She headed for the nearest in-house phone, answering her page. The extension was for the hospital switchboard. 'Dr Beresford.'

'Annie, Natasha's on the line for you,' the switchboard operator said.

'Thanks.' Annie waited while she was connected. 'Hey, Natasha.'

'Oh, Annie, I have some bad news.'

'What's wrong?' The urgency in her friend's voice made her feel uneasy.

'I've been up all night long with Rachael. She's been vomiting and now the boys are complaining of stomach-ache as well.'

'How's Lily?' Annie asked after their sixteen-year-old daughter.

'She slept over at a friend's last night so hopefully she's fine. I'm expecting her home in a few hours' time.'

'Monty's not sick?'

'No, but he's due on at the hospital soon and—'

'And you can't take sick kids over to my apartment to wait for the furniture to arrive,' Annie finished for her.

'I'm sorry.'

'Don't be. It's not your fault and, of course, you must keep them comfortable.'

'What will you do?'

'I'll ring the furniture store and see if they can give me an idea of when they might deliver.'

'They never do.'

'I know but I'm hoping. I might be able to sneak home during my lunch-break but as I'm due in Theatre soon, I have no idea when that might be.'

'How about your new neighbour? Professor Robinson.'

'No way!' The thought of asking the professor to supervise her furniture seemed a little too intimate for her liking. 'I'll call the superintendent at the apartments. He's a nice, agreeable man. I'm sure he'll be able to help out.'

'I'm really sorry, honey.'

'It's fine. Go and take care of the kids and I'll check later to see how they are.' She rang off and sighed heavily as she hung up the receiver. Why couldn't her life be simple? Just for a few minutes? Everything always seemed so…complicated.

She rang the furniture store and received the usual answer—they couldn't say when the delivery truck would get around to her place. Next, she rang the super and was relieved when he said it wouldn't be a problem.

As she breathed a sigh of relief, her pager sounded and she groaned. Well, at least she'd had half a millisecond of peace. She noted the number was that of Emergency Theatres which meant her fractured femur patient was ready for her attention.

The operation was routine but twice during her theatre

stint her pager beeped. The scout nurse called through to the number, informing them that Dr Beresford was in surgery. After the operation, Annie sat down to write up the notes while the nurses worked around her.

'I'm looking forward to meeting him,' one nurse said.

'A friend of mine, who used to work with him at Perth General, said he's gorgeous.'

'Really? When does he start?'

'Monday.'

Annie didn't usually listen to gossip but sat up a little straighter when she realised they were talking about Hayden Robinson.

'Excellent. Is he single?'

'Divorced.' The nurse was speaking in a low tone filled with excitement at passing on the gossip.

'Better and better,' the second nurse said with glee.

Annie stood and closed the casenotes. 'Thanks for your assistance during the operation,' she said to the nurses.

'Not a problem, Annie.' They both smiled before continuing with their tasks and their conversation. She walked out of the room and went to Recovery to deliver the casenotes and check on her patient.

Everything was fine and as she headed for the changing rooms, one of the gossiping nurses came out. 'Annie! You forgot your pager. It's just beeped again.'

'Oh, gee, thanks a bunch,' Annie joked. 'The thing hasn't stopped beeping at me all day.'

'Hey, your fault for becoming a doctor. I'm sure it never beeped that much when you were nursing.'

Annie smiled and shrugged. 'Guess I can't have everything.' As she headed out of Recovery, she checked her pager. Three different numbers. One extension was the ward, the other was A and E and the third was a mobile phone number she didn't recognise. She frowned, trying to think who it might be. She headed for the ward and answered the questions of the clinical nurse consultant. After that, she headed for Monty's office.

'You paged me?' she asked, strolling right in without bothering to knock.

'Hey, Annie.' Brenton sat behind his desk and finished filling in a form.

'How were the kids when you left?'

'Rachael had stopped vomiting, Joshua took over and Chris was starting to look quite green.'

'Oh, poor Natasha.'

'I've called Lily and told her to stay at her friend's place for a bit longer. Luckily, Aunt Jude came back from overseas a few weeks ago so at least Tash won't be on her own.'

'Let's hope you don't get it.'

'I think Tash might already have been exposed but we'll see what happens. Rachael only appears to have been sick for twenty-four hours and I've had quite a few people in through A and E this morning with similar symptoms.'

'Terrific.' Annie's tone was despondent. 'Now,' she sighed, 'I believe you paged me?'

'Yes. You forgot to fill in some paperwork regarding one of the fractured arms you set earlier this morning.'

'Sorry. That was when the patient with the fractured femur came in.'

'Never mind. I just thought I'd increase your paperwork.'

'Gee, thanks, mate.'

'No problem. I know how much you love it.' He grinned at her. 'So…Tash tells me you have an…*interesting* neighbour.'

'Oh, don't you start.'

'What's he like? Tash said you thought he was good-looking.'

'Don't you and your wife have *any* secrets?'

'Nope.'

Annie grinned back at him and shook her head. Her pager beeped. 'I just want to hurl this thing through a window,' she muttered as she checked the number. Brenton laughed and Annie frowned. 'It's the same number as before. Do you know this mobile phone number?' She recited it to her old friend but he shook his head.

'Only one way to find out,' he said and pushed the phone on his desk in her direction.

'Thanks.' Annie dialled the number and waited to be connected.

'Hello.' The deep voice on the other end of the line was brisk.

'This is Dr Beresford. I believe you were paging me?'

'Annie?'

'Yes?' She listened cautiously, trying to figure out who it was.

'It's Hayden Robinson.'

'Oh.' Eyes wide in surprise, she felt a tingle flood through her body. What on earth did he want?

'Your furniture has arrived and the delivery men want to know where you want things put or they'll just dump it anywhere they like. Also, do you have anything besides instant coffee? The movers were thirsty,' he added by way of explanation.

'Where's the superintendent?' She ignored his remark about the coffee.

'He had to go.'

'What!'

'What's wrong?' Brenton asked.

'I can help out,' Hayden continued, and for a second she thought she detected a hint of humour in his tone. 'At least that way things won't be left in the middle of the floor.'

'You're in my *apartment*?' she asked incredulously.

'Yes. The super left me in charge.'

'Excellent,' Annie mumbled gruffly. 'Fine. Look…' She checked her watch. 'I'll be there in five minutes.' She re-placed the receiver and momentarily covered her face with her hands. Taking a deep breath, she looked at Brenton. 'Listen, Monty, I have to step out for about twenty minutes.' She quickly told him what was going on.

'Well, that was nice of Professor Robinson to help out like that.'

'Yeah, right. Page me if you need me. Everyone else has.' She was turning to leave his office when he stopped her.

'Annie.' He threw her a set of keys. 'Take my car. It'll be quicker than trying to get a taxi.'

'Thanks, mate.' Annie rushed out to the doctors' car park and headed for Brenton's Jaguar XJ6. Exactly four minutes later, thanks to green lights all the way, she parked the car in the guest parking spot at her apartment building, just as the furniture delivery truck drove away.

'Great.' She climbed out of the car and locked the door. Taking the stairs two at a time, she rushed to her floor, noticing all the apartment doors were closed—including hers. 'Great.' Digging in her shorts pocket for her keys, she shoved one into the lock and opened the door.

There, in the middle of her living room, dressed in shorts and casual cotton shirt was Hayden Robinson. He seemed oversized, like an out-of-proportion cartoon character, in a room that was now filled with furniture. Arranged furniture, she realised. Things weren't all jumbled up as she'd imagined but instead everything was tastefully arranged. She couldn't have done it better herself.

Her gaze flicked around the room quickly before settling on Hayden once more. He'd looked up when she'd opened the door and she realised, belatedly, that he was holding something in his hand. A photo frame.

She looked down at his feet where one of her boxes had been knocked over, several items having fallen out onto the carpet, unravelling themselves from the protective paper. She recognised the one Hayden held in his hand. It was a silver frame with colourful love hearts around the border. It was the frame that currently held a picture of Adam. When they'd broken up, she'd relegated it to a bottom drawer but hadn't found the time to change the photograph.

Hayden looked at her—accusingly. She frowned, unsure why. He held out the photo frame so she could see the picture of the man she'd been engaged to.

'Why do you have a picture of my cousin?'

CHAPTER TWO

'YOUR *cousin*!'

Adam watched as the colour drained from Annie's face. 'Here.' He took her arm and guided her to a chair, gently pushing her down. 'Sit down before you fall down.' He caught a glimpse of her smooth legs as she sat, her khaki shorts hitching themselves higher. Very nice. Taking one last look at the photograph, he set it on her new bookshelf. 'Adam is my cousin. I'm just curious why you have his picture in a pretty love-heart frame.'

Hayden kept his tone neutral while his brain searched for a rational explanation. He hadn't seen Adam in years, but now that he'd moved back to the eastern coast of Australia he was planning to catch up with him soon—like this evening, if he could!

He looked down at Annie, wanting to sort this out—but as soon as he looked at her, he knew it was a mistake. She was at a disadvantage sitting down but it made him realise just how much of her skin was on show. Her white summer top revealed an expanse of lightly tanned skin around her neck and shoulders—skin that would no doubt be soft to touch. He shoved his hands into his pockets and sat down opposite her.

She pushed a trembling hand through her curls and he realised he'd unnerved her. 'How do you know Adam?'

'If you're his cousin, I'd expect you to know.'

Her tone was calm and he realised she was doing a great job of hiding her emotions. He nodded slowly. 'That's true but I haven't seen him in a while.'

'Then why don't you get him to tell you what happened?' She forced her legs to work and stood. Now that

23

she'd got over the initial shock of discovering Hayden was Adam's cousin, anger started to set in. How dared he question her? 'It's really none of your business.' She picked up the frame and stalked into the kitchen. She heard Hayden move and realised he'd followed her.

She turned to look at him and tossed the frame into the bin. 'End of discussion.'

'So you're just going to throw it out?' He leaned against the doorjamb, his gaze focused on her. 'Seems like your answer for anything that bothers you.'

'How dare you? You know nothing about me.'

'I know. That's what I'm trying to find out.' He stood up straight and advanced slowly into the kitchen. 'What was the deal…' he took a step closer '…with you…' another step '…and Adam?'

Annie swallowed, her gaze flicking between his lips and his mouth. 'It's none of your business.'

She was right. It wasn't, and his burning need to know the details of her relationship with his cousin surprised him. Why did it bother him so much? He was naturally distrustful of women, especially after his own ugly divorce, but why did he really care if she'd broken Adam's heart?

Because if she had, she was capable of breaking someone else's. He couldn't deny he'd been instantly attracted to Annie but he couldn't discount this information. She broke free of his gaze and started pacing up and down her kitchen, her arms crossed defensively over her chest before stopping next to the bin.

She was agitated and upset and he felt a stirring of guilt. 'Look, Hayden, this is my apartment and I'd appreciate it if you would leave. I don't have to explain anything to you, I don't have to stand here and answer your questions. Thank you for your help with my furniture but would you, please, leave?' When he didn't move, she tried again. 'At work you'll be my boss and that's a different issue, but right now I'd like you to leave.'

Without a word he took a small step towards her. Annie

automatically backed away, coming up hard against the
bench, her heart rate accelerating with awareness. Her eyes
were wide with surprise and her breath caught in her throat.
Hayden continued to advance. When he stood before her,
almost toe to toe, he reached down and pulled the frame
out of the bin, thankful there was nothing but paper in there.
Without glancing at it, he reached forward, his arm brush-
ing hers as he placed the item on the bench behind her.

He was close. So close she could feel his breath on her
cheek, smell the scent of him and feel the warmth emanat-
ing from his entire body. He exhaled slowly as he straightened. His gaze scanned her face, stopping for way too long
on her lips before returning to her eyes. There was one sure-
fire way to find out how deeply she felt towards his cousin
and the idea was certainly an intriguing possibility.

Annie felt as though she were about to burst an artery.
The magnitude of her situation settled over her. She was
close…*very* close to Hayden. If he edged just a little closer,
their bodies would be touching—which wasn't such an un-
appealing thought.

A rush of pent-up air escaped between her lips, making
them dry. Unconsciously, her tongue slipped out to wet
them, Hayden watching the action closely. She kept her
gaze fixed on his and was amazed to see the dark blue
depths clouding with…desire. Desire? The knowledge set
off an explosion of fireworks deep within her belly, their
heat warming her right the way through.

Surely she was mistaken. Men like Hayden Robinson
didn't find little mousy-brown women like herself desir-
able, yet when his hand came up to cup her cheek, his
thumb tenderly caressing her skin, she could take it no
longer. Her eyelids fluttered closed and she gave in to the
sensations he evoked. Her head felt light and fuzzy, incapable of any coherent thought except wanting Hayden's lips
on her own as soon as possible. What was it about this
man? No man had ever made her feel faint before.

A low, guttural sound came from him and a fraction of

a second later she felt him move away. Her eyelids snapped open and she could see the desire dying.

Common sense had won out.

Annie couldn't move.

'You're right.' His tone was deep, the repressed emotion still evident. 'It is none of my business—you and Adam.'

She needed space. She needed time to think and process the emotions she was feeling. She edged past him, ignored the small spark of need which shot through her, and stalked to the door. Wrenching it open, she indicated he should go.

Hayden nodded and walked to the door. She started to relax, thinking she was home and dry, but he stopped opposite her and her heart rate increased instantly. Slowly, a smile formed on his lips, one that was designed to melt even the hardest of hearts—and much to her disgust it was working.

'Don't be mad, Annie.'

'Why not?'

'Because we have to work together.'

'I've worked with many people I don't like and never had a problem.'

'But I'll bet they weren't your boss.'

She hated him for being right. Her pager started beeping and she groaned.

'One of those days?' he asked knowingly.

She nodded and checked her pager. 'I'm needed in A and E.' She patted her shorts pocket to check her keys were still there before looking up at him. 'Well, if you won't leave my apartment, I guess I will.' With that, she turned and walked towards the stairwell, determined not to look back but conscious of the fact that he watched her the entire way.

Hayden shook his head as the stairwell door closed. What on earth had he been thinking? He'd almost kissed her! He closed Annie's apartment door firmly behind him before stalking back to his own place. He paced around his living room, unsure why he felt so out of control.

He would be working with her, for heaven's sake. Not only that, but it appeared she was or had been involved with his cousin. He remembered her saying yesterday something about a bad break-up. Was Adam the person she'd recently broken up with?

'Adam.' He stalked to the phone and looked up his cousin's mobile number. Punching in the number with determination, he waited impatiently for his cousin to pick up the phone. When the voice mail clicked in, Hayden was stumped. What on earth was he supposed to say? Hi, Adam, do you know an Annie Beresford and what is your relationship with her? Why does my neighbour have your picture in a frame surrounded by love hearts? Is it serious? Do you love her?

Instead he growled, 'It's Hayden. Call me back.' He recited his number before hanging up. Adam had always had a way with the ladies. In fact, he clearly remembered back when they'd been hormone-ridden teenagers, Adam had usually had two or three girls on the go at one time. Was Annie another of his cousin's discarded pile? Was that why she'd reacted so defensively when questioned?

Hayden was a man who liked to have things straight—sorted out into nice, neat piles—and this was far from sorted. Annie would just say it was none of his business but, due to his unwanted attraction to her, it had become his business. Adam was his cousin. Annie was his registrar—*and* his neighbour.

He raked a hand through his hair as he realised his thoughts had come back to square one. He'd learnt long ago to keep his private life private—separate from the hospital. Now that Annie was living next door, how was he going to do that—especially when he was very much attracted to the petite dynamo?

Annie stopped by her favourite hang-out after her shift on Saturday—the pool hall. She loved it because it wasn't connected with the hospital or its staff. She greeted Trevor, the owner, with a warm hug. He was in his early forties, tall with long brown hair that curled around his shoulders and laughing brown eyes.

'G'day, handsome. How's business tonight?'

Trevor hugged her back. 'Not bad. A few new people in but, being Saturday night, it'll heat up soon. Drink?'

'Sure. A lemonade will be fine.'

'You got it. There's a new guy on table two. Looks like your type so why don't you go over and introduce yourself? You know, be friendly.'

'What do you mean, *my type*?'

'Annie—I *used to be* your type.'

Annie laughed. 'That was years ago, Trev.'

'Go and say hi at any rate. I want my customers to come back, not be ignored.'

'What if he *wants* to be ignored?' Annie peered over towards table two at the back of the large room and could see a man with his back to her, bent over as he lined up a shot.

'Will you just go?'

'All right.' She headed slowly towards table two, admiring the man's butt as he leaned over the table. Her gaze travelled up his body, over his firm back to his flexed triceps. She didn't want to disturb him while he took the shot so waited just off to the side. When he'd finished, Annie felt her jaw drop to the ground as he turned slightly to chalk his cue.

'Hayden!'

He spun around. 'Annie!'

'What are you doing here?' they said in unison and then laughed.

'Sorry.' She smiled at him. 'I see you've already found the best place to unwind in town.'

'Yes.' They stood staring at each other for a moment before he reached for the triangle and started racking the balls up. 'Care for a game?'

'Sure.'

'Do you come here often?'

'Yes, as a matter of fact.'

Trevor came over with her drink. 'Annie's been a regular here for about eight years now.'

Hayden raised his eyebrows in surprise. 'Interesting.'

'She's an interesting woman. Says coming here helps her unwind from her work. She's a doctor, you know.'

'Trevor,' Annie muttered, slightly embarrassed at the way her friend was all but pushing her on Hayden.

Hayden merely laughed. 'I know. Come Monday, we'll be working together.'

'You two know each other?'

'We're neighbours,' Annie supplied.

'Small world.' Trevor nodded and offered Hayden another drink.

'No, thanks.' With that, they were left to themselves again. 'How *was* the hospital today?'

Annie walked over to the wall which was lined with a row of chairs. 'Busy.' She put her briefcase and bag on the chair before heading to the cue rack. 'We have a new boss starting on Monday…' she chose a cue '…so we're trying to get everything shipshape and in order.' She leaned closer and said in a conspiratorial whisper, 'I hear he's a tyrant.'

Hayden nodded and matched her whisper. 'It's true.'

Annie laughed and looked into his eyes, wondering why she found him so intriguing. He was…different somehow from men she'd dated. Definitely different from Adam at any rate, even though they were cousins. Slowly the smile faded but their gazes remained locked.

'Hey, Annie,' someone called, and she quickly took a guilty step back and turned to look at who was addressing her.

'Hi, Angelo.' She waved back and waited while Angelo walked over. She introduced him to Hayden and after the two men had shaken hands, Angelo reminded her of a game she'd promised him.

'She's a doctor, you see,' he explained to Hayden, who

merely nodded. 'And right when I'm on a winning streak, she gets beeped with an emergency and has to go to the hospital. Right in the middle of a game!'

'Disgusting,' Hayden remarked. 'Doctors. They never play fair.'

'Hey, you said it, man.' Angelo held up his hand for a high five. 'So, what do *you* do, man?'

'I'm a doctor.'

Both Annie and Hayden laughed as Angelo lowered his hand at the news in obvious disgust. 'Then I ain't playing a game against you.'

'It's only when we're on call, Angelo. The rest of the time, it's not that bad.'

'Don't you believe her,' Trevor said as he walked over with Angelo's drink. 'Even though Annie was still nursing when I dated her, she was always running off to that place at the most inconvenient times.'

'You dated Annie?' Hayden was surprised.

'Yeah.' Trevor slung an arm around her shoulders. 'She's a great girl, our Annie, but as far as she and I were concerned, we made better friends than anything else. We've been friends since.'

'True. So, you ready to play, boss, or you going to bond with the guys some more?'

'Play.'

A few more people walked in and Angelo and Trevor went to greet them, leaving Annie and Hayden alone yet again.

'You can break,' he said, and when her cue was lined up to take the shot, he murmured, 'You and Trevor, eh?'

Annie wondered if he was trying to break her concentration but ignored him. 'Yup. Problem?'

'No. No. Not at all. He just doesn't seem…your type.'

Did everyone here know what her type was? 'It was a long time ago. Besides…' She rested her cue on the ground and shifted her weight. 'Who *is* my type? Adam?'

'No. I wouldn't say Adam was your type.'

'Because he's not.'

Hayden looked at her before bending down to take his turn. A ball shot into a pocket. 'You're not together any more?'

'No.'

He lined up another shot and then glanced across the table at her. 'Good.' He hit the ball without breaking his gaze from hers, neither of them moving until they heard the click as that ball joined the previous one he'd sunk.

On the inside Annie jumped for joy and squealed with delight at the top of her lungs. Outwardly she gave him a promising smile, her eyes lighting with glee. He *was* interested in her. She had no idea why but nevertheless he was interested. She watched as he prowled around the table, sizing up which ball would be his next victim.

Hayden potted one after another, never missing a trick, but Annie didn't care. She was on cloud nine. This gorgeous man was interested in her.

While they played a few games, they talked about life within the hospital, but Annie didn't tell him anything specific about the department. 'I like to keep this place separate from my hospital life.'

'Understood.' He sank the last ball and the game was over.

'Three games out of three. Congratulations.'

'I think you were letting me win. Either that or your mind wasn't on the game.'

'Probably the latter.' Annie put her cue away and picked up her bags. 'I'll definitely wipe the floor with you next time.'

'I have no doubt about that.' He checked his watch. 'Nine-thirty? I had no idea it was so late.' He glanced around at the rest of the tables which had slowly but surely started to fill up with patrons·playing and watching.

Annie chuckled. 'You sound old, Hayden. This place is only just starting to jump.'

'I have a phone call to make. Are you walking home?'

'Trevor usually makes me take a taxi if I'm here after dark.'

'Wise man.'

'But it's really nice and warm outside so I thought I might walk…*if* I could find a willing escort.' She looked pointedly at him.

'You're in luck. I happen to be free at the moment.'

'Good.' They headed out, waving to Trevor as they went. After the cool air-conditioning in the hall, the heat hit them slap bang in the face.

'Did you say it was *nice* out here?' Hayden remarked with a smile.

'Quit complaining and start walking. It's only a few blocks.'

'Would you like me to take your briefcase?'

'I've got it. It's not that heavy tonight.'

'Just you wait until Monday.'

Annie smiled, delighted with the way they were teasing and flirting with each other. She talked about Geelong, pointing the direction to a lot of its landmarks. 'The old wool shed is down there but now it's part of the university.'

'I know.'

'You do? I thought you were from Perth?'

'I've come here from Perth but I'm not as unfamiliar with the eastern side of Australia as you would think.'

'Really?'

'Yes. I was raised a Sydney boy and one of my sisters actually lives in Melbourne—well, Williamstown.'

'But this is your first time living in Victoria?'

'Yes.'

'Good. Then you can continue to play tourist and keep quiet.'

Hayden laughed. They were nearing their apartments and Annie felt the mood change from one of camaraderie to one of intense awareness. She smiled politely as he held the stairwell door for her, while her insides were churning with mounting anticipation.

They climbed the stairs in silence and walked out onto their floor. Annie stopped by her apartment door and turned to face him. 'Thanks for walking me home, Hayden.'

He shrugged. 'I was going your way.' The phone inside his apartment started ringing and he quickly unlocked his door. 'That'll be my sister, wondering why I haven't called her yet.'

Annie smiled as he rolled his eyes. 'Go answer it.'

'See you.' He disappeared into his apartment and once more Annie found herself standing out in the corridor, staring at his door.

'Shake it off,' she mumbled as she unlocked her own door and went inside. Once there, she dumped her bag and briefcase and allowed her excitement out. Doing a little dance, she took a deep breath and collapsed onto the lounge. Hayden Robinson was a gorgeous man who not only understood her profession but was involved in it, too.

Still, she needed to be cautious. She'd dated colleagues from the hospital before and when it hadn't worked out, she'd had to live with the gossip. *If* anything was going to happen between herself and Hayden, would they be able to keep it secret from the hospital grapevine?

Steady on, girl. You hardly know him and come Monday you may change your mind if he really is a tyrant to work for. Sobering her thoughts once more, she went to the kitchen to make something to eat, only then realising just how hungry she was…and not just for food.

Monday morning dawned bright and early and Annie was sick and tired of wrestling with sleep. Her stomach was in knots and her head was pounding with excitement. Today was the day. Today Hayden became her boss. She'd only met him three days ago but it felt like…for ever.

She walked into the kitchen and switched the kettle on. Hopefully, a cup of coffee might help the dull ache she felt at the back of her head. She glanced to where Adam's picture still stood on the bench where Hayden had put it on Saturday.

She'd thought about that 'almost kiss' a lot more during the past forty-eight hours. When she'd been finishing off her paperwork on Sunday, when she'd gone out for a run, when she'd scrubbed her apartment from top to bottom and when she'd gone shopping to buy more glasses.

She'd thought about him more than she cared to admit. What was it about the man which drew her so completely she forgot all rational thought?

She grabbed the photo frame, undid the back and took out Adam's picture. Looking down at his smiling face, she tried to figure out what she'd ever seen in him. It was then she realised she was also looking for a family resemblance to Hayden. Were they really cousins?

'It doesn't matter.' She tossed the picture into the bin and made herself a cup of instant coffee. The chapter in her life devoted to Adam was well and truly finished. With an importance she couldn't rationalise, she stalked into the living room and began sorting through some boxes. Finally, she found what she'd been looking for. Another photograph. One of the Worthington family. It was the right size and with great relish she put it into the frame before setting it on top of her bookshelf.

'Much better.' After drinking her coffee, she checked the clock—almost six in the morning. She didn't start work until eight so with some time to kill she changed into a pair of running shorts and top, slapped on some sunscreen, sunglasses, shoes and a hat and checked she had her keys before heading out for a run.

The streetlights were still on even though the sun was only starting to peek over the horizon. Not much traffic was on the roads and the breeze was already quite warm. Then again, the beginning of January was usually pretty hot. Annie jogged along the running track, focusing on calming down her thoughts.

At the moment they were so mixed up she doubted she

remembered her name. Ever since meeting him last Friday,
Hayden had been constantly on her mind *and* the major
cause of her sleep deprivation. The 'almost kiss' they'd
shared, the flirting at the pool hall—everything—just
played over and over in her mind like a stuck record.

She shook her head, trying to clear the image of desire
she'd seen in his eyes. Was it real? Was he interested in
just fooling around or interested in a serious commitment?
Relationship? He'd already been divorced once—had that
put him off marriage completely?

As her feet continued to eat up the footpath, her thoughts
continued, trying to get a firm grip on her present reality.
She was almost forty and knew for a fact that her biological
clock was definitely ticking. If her knight in shining armour
didn't come along soon, she…she didn't want to think
about it. He *had* to come. He just *had* to.

Annie turned around and headed back towards her apartment, a scowl fixed on her face as she concentrated on the
ground in front of her.

'Oof.' She ran straight into someone else, knocking them
both off balance, her sunglasses and hat coming off in the
process. 'Ugh.' She landed on the ground with a thud, her
right knee and elbow stinging instantly. 'Ow.' She was
sprawled over some man and when she lifted her head she
felt a bubble of hysterical laughter rise up within her.
'Hayden!'

'Annie!' He was equally astounded. 'We have got to stop
running into each other.'

'Literally,' she added on a laugh as she quickly disen-
tangled herself from him, working hard to stop herself from
committing every contour of his body to memory. They
both picked themselves up. 'Are you all right?'

She looked down at her knee, seeing blood oozing
slightly. 'Fine. It's just a graze. Sorry about that. I wasn't
watching where I was going.'

'Same here. I… It's usually empty along here at this time

of the morning.' He looked at her more closely. 'Have you already been to the end?'

'Yes.' She shrugged and, needing something to do, bent to pick up her sunglasses and hat. 'I…er…couldn't sleep.'

'Nervous?'

'About?'

'Working with me.'

Annie lifted her chin defiantly, her eyes sparking with challenge. 'What if I am?'

Man, he liked it when she looked at him like that. She was so…*alive*. He swallowed over the emotion and leaned a little closer. 'You needn't be. I'm a good surgeon and I know how to run a department.'

'But you were having trouble running along a path.'

He laughed. 'That's different and you know it.'

Why did he have to laugh? It wasn't fair. Her heart pounded out an erratic rhythm which had nothing to do with her early morning exercise. 'I'm sure you're good at your job…'

'But?'

'But…' she shrugged '…change is always hard to accept.'

'Meaning?'

She looked away, down at the ground, the silence stretching. 'I have to go.' She gestured to her knee. 'I don't want to spoil your run.'

'It's OK. I'll walk back with you.'

'I'll be fine.' She waved his concern away. He looked so incredibly handsome right now and it was all she could do *not* to throw herself into his arms.

'I'm ready to head back anyway.'

She raised an eyebrow. 'You're probably right. An old man like you couldn't make it to the end and back.'

He surprised her by laughing. 'Why didn't I think to bring my wheelchair?'

Annie smiled and inclined her head in the direction

they'd be walking. 'Let's go, then.' She winced slightly as they started, her knee stinging.

'You sure you're OK?'

'I did worse in the school yard growing up.'

He chuckled. 'I sense there's a story behind your slightly crooked nose.'

'You sense correctly.' Annie touched her nose a little self-consciously, the light-hearted moment evaporating.

'What happened?'

'Ah…it's a long, boring story. Not of interest.'

'OK.'

'I take it you like the beach,' she commented. Hayden frowned at her, slightly puzzled. 'I'm just trying to find a nice, safe, neutral topic of conversation.'

'Ah. Yes, I like the beach. It…relaxes me.'

'Me, too.' She winced again, starting to feel a few more aches and pains throughout her body where they had collided. 'Do you surf?'

'Yes, when I get the time for it.'

'I've never tried it.'

'So what do you like to do to relax?' The instant he'd said the words, he realised how they could be misconstrued.

Annie glanced up at him, a small smile forming on her lips. His voice had been husky as he'd asked the question and her smile increased when he quickly cleared his throat. The urge to tease him was great but, due to her stinging knee and bruised elbow, she decided to let him off the hook…just this once. 'I like to snorkel, swim. Running is a good way to unwind—well, it is when I don't crash into people.'

Hayden laughed. 'Agreed. Snorkelling's good. Have you been to the Great Barrier Reef?'

'Many times, and still I'm always in awe of its beauty.'

They'd reached the apartment block. 'Think you can manage the stairs or do you want to take the lift?'

'Stairs are fine.' He held the door open to the stairwell and frowned a little as Annie winced when she started climbing the stairs. When they reached their floor, he surprised himself by asking her in for coffee.

'Uh…' Annie wasn't too sure.

'Come on. It's just coffee—*real* coffee, by the way. And besides, you haven't told me about the department yet.' He unlocked his door and opened it, indicating she should go inside.

'I couldn't do that. It would be like giving information to the enemy.' She peered through the open door, unsure what might be on the other side.

'Is that how you see me?'

'Kind of,' she replied a little absent-mindedly as she walked past him, making sure their bodies didn't touch. The layout of the apartment was identical to hers but was sparsely decorated. A large desk was set up in one corner with a computer on it. Two luxurious chairs were in the centre of the room with a coffee-table between them, and a bookcase filled to the brim was in the corner.

'Have a seat,' he offered. She sat in the proffered chair which completely enveloped her, her feet unable to touch the ground. 'Coffee should be ready soon.' He headed to the kitchen and she struggled to sit forward, feeling like a little girl with her legs dangling. She'd just finished composing herself when he returned…and surprised her again by kneeling at her feet.

'What are you doing?' she demanded.

He opened a small medicine kit. 'House call.'

'But this isn't my house.'

'Annie.'

'It's fine, Hayden.'

'I don't want blood all over my carpet.'

'Then you shouldn't have asked me in.'

'Tell me about the department. Why would you see me as an enemy?'

'Not an enemy as such.'

'Go on.' He ripped open an antiseptic towel and started to clean her knee. She winced slightly but that was all.

'Good girl. If you're really brave, you can have two cups of coffee.'

'Gee, thanks.'

'The department,' he prompted.

'Brian Newton, your predecessor, was in charge of the orthopaedic department since its initial inception fifteen years ago. Before that it had been attached to the surgical department.'

'People are used to his ways and his only,' Hayden stated.

'Yes. He's a nice man, Brian, and we'd all do anything for him.'

'Can't ask for better than that with staff.'

'I'm not saying that you'll do—ow—things wrong, it's just that— Ow, Hayden.' He was spraying something on her knee. 'That stuff stings.'

He raised an eyebrow. 'For a doctor, you're mighty vocal when it comes to being a patient.'

'Have you ever thought it might be your bedside manner?' Annie had made the remark in all innocence yet in that instant she realised he might take it another way.

'I see. Am I not being gentle enough with you? I'm simply trying to be thorough and make sure you don't have any bits of dirt or gravel left where they can fester and rot.'

'Charming. Do I still get my second cup of coffee?'

'It's debatable.' Hayden looked briefly at her elbow, which only had a slight graze. He sprayed some stinging stuff on it before finishing off her knee. He stuck a sticking plaster over the graze and then, to her surprise, bent his head and kissed it. 'All better,' he pronounced, and before she could say another word he'd gathered up his medical supplies and walked from the room.

Annie covered her face with her hands and leaned back into the chair, practising some deep, calming breaths. At this rate, she'd need another run to calm herself down. She stood up, a little too quickly, and grimaced in pain. This was not a good start to the day. She intended to do something to improve it by leaving Hayden's apartment—immediately. She limped towards the door.

'Where do you think you're going?' He used his best doctor voice.

Annie turned around and pointed to the wall. 'Home.'

'But we haven't had coffee yet.'

'Uh… I know. I think I'll take a rain-check, Hayden.'

'Sit down, Annie. At least give your knee a few more minutes of rest. After all, you *are* going to be on it all day.'

He had a point. Without waiting for her answer, he disappeared again and she could hear him taking cups out of the cupboard. Moments later he carried through a tray with two cups of coffee and some sweet rolls. She'd perched herself on the edge of the chair, not wanting to get lost in it again.

'You look as though you were expecting company this morning,' she stated, wondering if he'd set her up. He could have seen her leave her apartment and decided he'd lure her back here to…to do what? All he'd done had been to ask her about the department. So far…

'Not at all. My sister brought them around yesterday when she came to visit.' He helped himself to a roll and took a bite. She waited while he chewed and swallowed. 'They're cinnamon rolls and I've just put them in the microwave for a few seconds to heat them up—as per Katrina's instructions.'

'Oh.' Annie took a cup off the tray, taking a sip of the strong black coffee. 'Nice.'

He followed suit and then stopped. 'Did you want any milk or sugar? I drink mine black so I just made yours the same. Sorry, I should have asked.'

She smiled. 'It's fine.' She took another sip as though to prove it.

They both fell silent.

Annie searched wildly for something to say. What had they been talking about before? Blank. Her mind was blank. All she was conscious of was the way Hayden looked sit-

ting opposite her, his body relaxed in the chair, his long,
tanned legs stretched out and crossed at the ankles and his
feet most definitely touching the floor. He'd obviously had
these chairs made to suit his over six-foot stature. Needing
something to do, she took a plate and helped herself to one
of the cinnamon rolls.

'You look uncomfortable. Sit back. These chairs are glorious to relax in.'

She smiled. 'I'm sure they are.' She broke off a piece of
the roll and popped it in her mouth. All she could focus on
was his lean body, firm and taut and on view just for her.
She glanced up to meet his gaze and realised he was aware
of her scrutiny. He raised a quizzical eyebrow but didn't
say anything. Instead, he took another bite of his roll and
swallow of his coffee.

The atmosphere was growing more tense with each passing second. Why couldn't she think of anything to say?
Why did his close presence have such an effect on her?
Why had she picked up the roll in the first place? Although
it was delicious, she now had to eat it and she was the type
of person to drop crumbs on her clothes—something she
didn't want to do in front of Hayden.

He swallowed his mouthful and put his plate and cup on
the table. 'Eat up. They're delicious, aren't they?' he stated.

'Yes. Your sister's a good cook.' Good grief! Could her
conversation get any more stilted?

'I think today will be very interesting. Naturally, it'll take
me a while to settle in. I'm quite prepared for that and, of
course, I'll want to put my own stamp on the department.
If that puts people's noses out of joint then so be it. The
way I see it, they're stuck with me until they finish their
rotation, or if they're secretarial staff, they can transfer.'
Hayden laced his hands behind his head and leaned back
in the chair. He shouldn't have done that because it made
his biceps flex beneath his T-shirt. Annie choked on the
mouthful she was eating and started to cough. 'You OK?'

Annie smiled placatingly, waving away his concern as

she swallowed, coughed and reached for her coffee. Taking a sip, she looked up at him, knowing her face would almost be the colour of beetroot. 'I'm fine,' she whispered, her voice a little hoarse. She cleared her throat and tried again. 'I'm fine.'

She placed her plate and cup on the table and stood. 'I really think I should go. Time's ticking and I have a few more things to do before I head to the hospital.' She thought for a moment he was going to try and waylay her again but he merely nodded and walked her to the door. 'Thanks for the coffee—oh, and the roll. Please, tell your sister I thought they were delicious.'

He nodded. 'Hope your knee's better and I'll see you at the hospital.'

'Yes.' She walked past him, holding her breath so she didn't breathe in the clean, earthy scent that surrounded him.

'Do you walk?'

She frowned at him. 'Yes.' Couldn't he see she was walking?

'To the hospital,' he clarified with a smile.

'Usually.'

Hayden nodded again, and when he didn't say anything else she forced a smile and quickly hobbled to her own apartment. Thankfully, he didn't wait for her to open her own door and once his was shut, she started to relax a little. Fumbling with her keys, she finally put the correct one in the lock and stumbled through the door.

Leaning against it, Annie closed her eyes, trying to figure out who she was and where the coherent, professional woman she used to be had gone.

CHAPTER THREE

When Annie walked through the hospital doors at seven-thirty, it was to find Hayden standing in the main A and E corridor, shaking hands with Brenton.

'Hey, Annie.' Brenton beckoned her over and put an arm about her shoulders, smiling down at her.

'Annie will be a big help to you, I'm sure. One smart woman.'

She glanced up at her friend. 'Stop it, Monty, you're making me blush.'

'That's what I'm here for.'

'Monty?' Hayden queried.

'Nickname,' Brenton answered. 'We've known each other since high school.'

'Really?'

'Well, I have some casenotes awaiting my attention before ward round so I'd better get to work.'

Brenton laughed. 'Yes. Don't want to get on the wrong side of the boss on his first day here.'

Annie's gaze flicked to meet Hayden's before she quickly looked away. 'See you on the ward.'

'I'll go with you.' He held out his hand to Brenton. 'Nice to meet you. Thanks for the welcome.'

'No problem.'

Annie knew she had to wait for Hayden. It would be bad manners not to and several staff were watching them closely. She strode through A and E, heading towards the orthopaedic ward and her cubby-hole, which hospital administration called an office. She stopped at the top of the ward. 'This is the orthopaedic ward and your office is down there.' She pointed to the right.

43

'I've already had a tour.'

'Then, if you'll excuse me, Professor, I need to get to work.' Without waiting for him to answer, she headed off. It wasn't until she'd unlocked her office and opened the door that she realised he'd followed her. He urged her inside and came in after her.

Her office wasn't big, by any stretch of the imagination. Room for a desk, chair and a filing cabinet. With Hayden standing, towering over her, she stepped back as far as she could, only to find herself up against the wall.

'Problem?'

'No. I was just wondering if Brenton was another previous boyfriend.'

'Pardon?'

'Well, so far we've had Adam and Trevor, and you've known Brenton since high school so I thought—'

'So you thought he was another of my discard pile?'

'I wouldn't put it like that exactly. We all have a past.'

'Yes.'

'Look, Annie, I'll be honest. I just want to know if there's a Mr Right in your life at the moment.'

She was stunned and couldn't speak.

He glanced at his watch. 'Annie? Not that I'm trying to pressure you or anything, but we have ward round soon and the rest of the day is going to be hectic so I wanted to get this sorted out now.'

'What sorted?'

'Are you seeing anyone?'

'No.'

The smile he turned on her was the sexiest she'd seen on him yet. 'Good.' It was the same look he'd given her in the pool hall on Saturday night—the one that had her jumping for joy on the inside. 'See you on the ward.'

She nodded, incapable of speech. He left her room and she slumped down into the chair, positive her legs wouldn't hold her up any longer. How on earth was she supposed to get through the rest of the day? She'd have to ignore him as best she could, otherwise she'd be stirring up a hornets' nest of gossip.

She worked hard at ignoring Hayden while doing the ward round…which didn't really work too well as she had to discuss the patients with him. She was polite and professional—anything else would have attracted attention and that was the last thing she wanted.

Once ward round was done, she headed to the clinic, knowing she'd be bumping into him for the rest of the day and trying to figure out the best way to cope. His questions had confused her. Did he want to date her? Was he looking for a relationship? Did he just want to get to know her as a colleague? Why was he so interested to find out if there was another man in her life? Her head was spinning.

After saying good morning to the clerical and nursing staff, Annie took the casenotes of a patient and called him in. She knew she was breaking protocol. As the senior registrar, it really was up to her to introduce Hayden but right now…right at this very moment she'd had enough of Hayden Robinson and the way the nurses and every other female he'd come into contact with so far that morning had fallen over him like lovesick schoolgirls.

After she'd reviewed the X-rays of her patient's fractured wrist and sent him off to have his cast removed, she wrote up the notes and headed back to the corridor.

'Annie. There you are.' It was Wesley, one of her fellow registrars and one of her least favourite people. His entire mindset was based on getting ahead by any possible means and if that meant jumping through a ring of fire into a cesspit of dog food, he would do it if his boss so ordered. 'You were rather quick off the mark today,' he remarked as he stood beside her, idly flicking through casenotes.

'There's a lot to get done.'

'I agree. I'm just surprised you left it up to me to introduce Professor Robinson to the rest of the clinic staff when it was really your job.'

'Surely you didn't mind,' Annie remarked. 'After all, I

know how you love to…ingratiate yourself with your superiors, Wesley.' She smiled sweetly as she said the words. 'No doubt Professor Robinson already counts you as a great asset.'

Wesley preened, Annie's sarcasm completely lost on him. 'You think so? Excellent.' He smiled and headed into a clinic room. Annie shook her head and called through another patient. She managed to see another four patients before someone knocked on her consulting-room door.

Without waiting for her permission, the door opened and Hayden walked in. He nodded politely to her patient and took a look at the X-rays on the viewing box. She finished writing up her notes and spoke reassuringly to her patient before introducing Hayden. The patient seemed happy to know the new Professor was interested in all his patients and left on her crutches, a happy camper.

'Is there something I can help you with, Professor?' Annie pasted a smile onto her lips.

'No need to put on an act here, Annie. It's just the two of us.'

'What do you want, Hayden?'

'I have a patient in my consulting room who is asking to see you.'

'Why didn't you just send him up to me? Or call me to come and take a look?'

'Now, where would be the fun in that?'

'This is medicine, Professor. It's not supposed to be fun.'

'You sound like a med school lecturer.'

'So who's this patient you want me to see?'

He opened her consulting-room door and together they marched down the corridor. 'Tobias Andersen.'

'Ah, yes. Mr Andersen. He always insists on seeing two doctors. Brian and I used to review him together as it saved time.'

'Good. We'll keep it that way.' He pushed open his consulting-room door, waiting for Annie to precede him.

'Actually, as you're more qualified than I am,' she said softly, 'it's protocol that you precede me.'

'Just get in there,' he grumbled good-naturedly. Annie smiled, delighted that a few minutes in Hayden's presence had overpowered her earlier confusion. She loved teasing and flirting with him as it made her feel…special.

'Good morning, Mr Andersen.'

'There you are, Dr Beresford, and it's about time, too.'

'Sorry for the delay,' Annie placated her patient. Mr Andersen was eighty-five years old, had broken almost every bone in his body at some point in his life and took great delight in recounting every single break at every appointment. He was now riddled with rheumatoid arthritis and had recently refractured his hip.

'I was in the middle of telling your new professor here all about the time I broke all the toes on my left foot when he rudely left the room. Kids these days,' Mr Andersen mumbled.

Hayden's eyebrows hit his hairline.

'Now, I'm sure you're exaggerating, Mr Andersen. Professor Robinson is a most polite man and I'm one hundred per cent positive he told you he was going to get me. Hadn't you been asking to see me?'

'Well, yes, when I got in here, but I was in the middle of a story.'

'Why don't you finish it now?' Hayden suggested. 'I'm sure Dr Beresford would love to hear it as well. While you're talking, we'll get you up onto the examination couch.'

That was all the encouragement Mr Andersen required and after Hayden had tested the man's range of hip movement as well as checking the wound site where Annie had performed the operation four weeks ago, they helped him off the couch.

'The wheel on your walker is a little crooked, Mr Andersen,' Annie noted, and picked up the phone. 'Just have a seat while I organise a replacement for you.'

With the phone cradled to her ear, she filled in the necessary paperwork for the new walker. Usually, it would take a few days for the request to be processed but, after working in this hospital for almost ten years, Annie knew the unofficial way to get things done.

Hayden half listened to Mr Andersen's story about how he'd received two fractures to his skull. The other half of him was overly conscious of Annie, her scent, her charm and, most of all, what she was saying on the phone. He knew how bad hospital red tape could be and he also knew how a crooked wheel on a walker could cause Mr Andersen to have yet another nasty fall.

'Thanks, Buddy. The usual arrangement? I'll make sure it's with you before lunch. Bye.' She rang off and tore off the top copy off the request she'd written out. 'Here you are, Mr Andersen. If you take this down, they'll swap your walker over immediately. Make sure you ask for Buddy.'

'I wouldn't have anyone else, Dr Beresford.' He stood and shuffled his way to the door. Annie looked at his gait, happy with the way he was now walking. 'I'll see you both in two weeks' time, then.'

'Absolutely, and I'll make sure the clinic staff schedule you to see us both.'

'Good-oh,' he replied, and shuffled through the door Annie held open for him. She closed it and headed back to Hayden's desk, ripping off the second form from the request book and putting it into an internal mail envelope. The final copy remained in the request book.

'Hospitals are the same the world over,' Hayden remarked as he watched her. 'Paperwork, red tape and long corridors.'

'And patients.'

'Really? Patients? Hmm. Yes, I guess so. Incidentally, what's the ''usual arrangement''?'

Annie smiled. 'Trade secret. If you're good and prove your worth here as head of our unit, I might let you in on the secret.'

His mouth curved into a slow smile. 'If you don't want to tell me, don't. I'll figure it out.'

Annie laughed. 'Good luck to you, Hayden. I'd better get back to—' There was a knock at Hayden's door and he quickly called for the person to come in. Wesley came through the door and stopped dead when he saw Annie.

He glared at her before turning his gaze to Hayden. 'I'm terribly sorry to disturb you, Professor Robinson.'

'Not at all. Come right in.' Hayden's joviality made Wesley's eyes narrow for a moment, as though he wasn't quite sure what had been going on but that he didn't like it one little bit.

'Thanks, Prof,' Annie called as she walked out the door, leaving Hayden to deal with Wesley. She saw a few more patients before telling the sister she had to step out for a minute. Racing down to the small shop at the front of the hospital, Annie bought some chocolate frogs and raced them around to Buddy.

'Payment, as per usual.'

'And delivered with that beautiful smile of yours. Thanks, Annie.'

'No. Thank you, Buddy. Hey, how's your aunt?'

'She's doing marvellously. She has no pain in her wrist any more, thanks to you.'

'Hey, that's what friends are for. I'd better get back to clinic.' Annie raced up the stairs, taking them two at a time, almost colliding with Brenton at the top.

'Steady on there, Annie. Where's the fire?'

'Have to get back to clinic. Just paying a chocky frog debt.' She slowed her pace a little and walked quickly through the open stairwell door into the corridor.

'Hey, you borrowed my car the other day. Why don't I get chocolate frogs?' Brenton called.

Annie kept walking but turned to smile at him over her shoulder. 'Wasn't patient related, Monty,' she called back. 'Ugh.' She'd walked into someone and looked up into

Hayden's blue eyes. His hands reached out to steady her and she felt the warmth of his nearness flood through her.

'This is getting to become a habit,' he drawled quietly.

'Sorry,' she mumbled, trying not to breathe deeply for fear she'd melt into his arms as her senses were overpowered by his delicious scent. Every nerve ending in her body zinged to life and she quickly stepped back.

'Chocolate frogs, eh?' The grin on his lips was triumphant.

'The hospital revolves around chocolate frogs.' She shrugged. 'It's the unofficial currency.'

'I'll remember that.'

'Where are you going?'

'Theatre. You're coming, too.'

'Me? No. It's not my day. Wesley operates on Mondays so you should be doing the list with him.'

'I've already spoken to him. I've changed it.'

'But—'

'You're the senior registrar, Dr Beresford. It's your duty to show me around on my first day.'

'Yes, but—'

'And you've already been negligent in your duties, not introducing me to staff here in Outpatients.'

Annie put her hands on her hips. 'Are you going to relent on this?'

Hayden's smile was smug. 'No.'

'Fine. Theatres are this way.' As they walked, Annie thought of the way Wesley would have reacted to the news that Hayden had switched the responsibility for the elective list. Oh, well, the man didn't like her so this was just one more reason.

'How did Wesley take the news?'

'He seemed fine with it. Why?'

'Nothing.'

'Come on, Annie. I can tell you're holding out on me.'

'That all depends who I'm speaking to. My friend or my boss?'

'Why can't I be both?'

Annie laughed. 'Oh, Hayden, you really have a good sense of humour.'

'All right. I'm your friend. Whatever you tell me, I promise it won't affect our working relationship.'

Annie shook her head but smiled at him. 'It's no great secret. Wesley resents me. I'm a woman.'

'And you're his superior.' Hayden nodded. 'When he's annoyed, does he clench his jaw?'

'Yes.'

'I'd say he was annoyed, then, but I made it clear it was only for today. Next week everything will be back to normal. I also told him he was more than welcome to join us in Theatre once he'd finished in Outpatients.'

'How kind of you, oh, gracious and wise professor,' Annie teased as they entered the theatre department, giving him no time to comment. She introduced him to the staff and showed him around before they changed and began to scrub.

The theatre list wasn't too hectic, with two knee arthroscopies, one fractured tarsus and a tibia which required external fixation. Annie performed the first arthroscopy, conscious of the fact that Hayden was watching her. Once she was finished she glanced up into his blue eyes and was relieved to find them twinkling with a smile.

'Did I pass the test?' she asked as she sat down to write up the operation notes. The theatre sister and another nurse were getting the theatre ready for the next patient.

'Yes.'

'So you admit you were testing me.'

'Of course.' He walked a little closer to her, his voice dropping to a low murmur as he peered over her shoulder to the casenotes in front of her. 'How am I supposed to know what to expect from you if I don't take close notice of how you do things? Neat handwriting, too. Good to know.'

The warmth generating from him passed through to her

and for a moment her mind went completely blank. She glanced down at the words she'd been writing and everything blurred together. She closed her eyes for a moment, trying to control her body's instant reaction to his nearness. 'Um…' She thought hard for something to say. What had they been talking about? Oh, that's right, handwriting. 'How's yours?'

'Illegible.'

He took a step away and she silently thanked him for it. 'Ah, the standard requirement to become a doctor—illegible handwriting.'

'Yes, I'm surprised they let you pass your final exams with such neat writing.'

'But I used to be a nurse.'

'Of course. Well, I guess they couldn't blame you for that.'

Annie turned and gave his shoulder a friendly punch. He laughed and took another step away. 'Leave nurses alone. They're wonderful people and under-appreciated by most doctors.' She said her spiel with a smile and a lot of laughter in her voice.

'Down, girl. I am not one of those doctors.'

'You tell him, Annie,' the theatre sister added.

'Nurses are…' Hayden paused, as though deep in thought. 'Nurses are…' he tried again, pretending he wasn't quite sure what nurses really were!

'Brilliant.' Annie supplied.

'Giving,' the theatre sister contributed.

'Always picking up after the doctors,' another nurse said.

'No. No. That's not what I was going to say.' Hayden looked at Annie, the teasing light dying from his eyes for a moment. 'Nurses are…special,' he finished with sincerity.

Annie felt her throat go dry. Why did he have to be so cute and sincere like that? It only endeared him to her more and that was the *last* thing she wanted right now. She glanced at the two other nurses in the room and both were looking at him as though he'd hung the moon.

'Which is probably why you needed to become a doctor, Annie. Nursing's far too special for you.'

'You rotten man.' Anne took a swipe at him again. He laughed and moved quickly out of her range. The other nurses laughed as well and Annie joined in.

'This looks…cosy,' Wesley said as he swung through the theatre door. His gaze narrowed on Annie but she smiled sweetly at him before returning her attention to the notes in front of her.

'You're just in time for the next arthroscopy, Wesley,' Hayden said. He turned to the theatre sister. 'Almost ready?'

'Yes, Prof.'

'Excellent.' Hayden walked over to Wesley. 'Why don't we go scrub because I'd like you to do the operation and I'll assist.'

'What? Right now?'

Annie had finished writing in the casenotes and watched as Wesley started to pale.

'Yes.'

'What about Dr Beresford? I thought she was doing this list with you.' There was the slightest hint of panic in his tone.

'She is, and now that you're here, you are, too. I've already watched Annie operate so now it's your turn. It shows me how well you cope with the pressure of being watched. It will stand you in good stead as you continue with your training.'

'Of course,' Wesley replied, as though getting a hold of himself. Annie watched as the two men went out to the scrub room, Hayden firmly in control of the situation.

'I thought all doctors liked to show off their skills?' the nurse remarked.

'They do. I think our new prof caught Wesley by surprise,' the theatre sister responded.

'But Annie was caught by surprise, too.'

'True.' Both women looked at Annie as she shut the

casenotes and stood. 'Annie's not only an ex-nurse but a woman as well,' the theatre sister remarked proudly. 'We're used to pressure.'

Annie smiled. 'Thanks for the vote of confidence.'

'Speaking of confidence…' The theatre sister came a little closer to Annie. 'You and the new professor seem quite relaxed with each other. Have you worked with him before?'

'No, but I wish I had.'

'Why? Because he's such a good-looking guy?'

Annie laughed. 'No. It's because his reputation as a brilliant surgeon has preceded him. I'm looking forward to seeing him operate this afternoon.'

'If he stops testing you,' the nurse added.

'Quite.' Annie nodded her head and walked out the door before either woman could ask more questions. She wasn't sure whether Hayden wanted her in Theatre while Wesley operated and hoped he'd say no. That way she could do a bit more paperwork and also take a break from being in his presence.

She walked out to the scrub sink and Hayden's gaze met hers. His eyes were mesmerising and Annie's step faltered. She looked down, desperately trying to pull herself together as she continued over to him.

'I'll just go and do some paperwork.'

'No.'

'Prof, you don't need me in Theatre while Wesley operates. I'll get Theatre Sister to give me a call when you're ready to do the fixator.'

'No. I'd like you to assist Wes so I can see how the two of you operate together.'

Annie watched as Wesley scowled at being called 'Wes'. No one called him that and if she wasn't so annoyed with Hayden, who was deliberately being pertinacious, she'd have been hard-pressed not to smile.

'I thought *you* were going to assist me, Professor Robinson,' Wesley interjected.

'I've changed my mind.'

It seemed there was nothing she could do about it so she shrugged her shoulders. 'Fair enough.' She joined him at the scrub sink. 'But I thought it was a *woman's* prerogative to change her mind.'

'Are you suggesting there's something feminine about me, Dr Beresford?' Hayden raised a quizzical eyebrow in a silent dare.

Annie felt her heart rate increase, her throat dry up as her gaze roved over him quickly. 'Uh…' She cleared her throat. 'No.'

'I'm very pleased to hear it. Right. Let's get this next patient done.'

Annie was relieved when Hayden and Wesley left the scrub sink because the embarrassment which flamed her entire body would have been enough to light up the hospital for a week! How could she have teased him like that—*and* in front of Wesley? She closed her eyes as she continued to scrub.

It was all Hayden's fault. Until he'd appeared in her life, everything had been rolling along smoothly. Well, if you could call having a broken engagement and your place burn down *smooth*, but still, at least her heart rate had remained at a more normal level. Now…now she wasn't sure what was happening, but it had started the moment she'd laid eyes on Hayden Robinson.

By the time she entered Theatre, Wesley was ready to begin. With great force she mentally pushed all thoughts of the man who was standing just to the side of her out of her head, which wasn't at all easy. The operation was completed without complications and she smiled behind her mask as Wesley visibly relaxed once he'd finished.

'Well done,' was all Hayden said. The rest of the list continued, with Hayden performing the remaining surgery, Wesley assisting him with the foot operation and Annie doing the tibia, which was the more complex out of the two.

'Thank you, everyone,' Hayden said both to Annie, Wesley and the rest of the theatre staff. 'If anyone needs me, I'll be in my office for the rest of the day. That is, if I can find my way back there.' He smiled good-naturedly. Everyone laughed.

'I'd be more than happy to show you, Professor Robinson,' Wesley said eagerly.

'Thank you, Wes.' He turned and looked at Annie. 'But I believe it's Dr Beresford's duty to show me around today. You've already covered for her once. You can't go making it a habit.'

Wesley seemed a little put out but heeded Hayden's words. 'Quite true.'

Both men looked at Annie and she rolled her eyes. 'Well, Hayden, what are you waiting for, then? Go and get changed and I'll meet you at the front of Theatres.'

He smiled. 'What a wonderful bedside manner you have, Doctor.'

The urge to poke her tongue out at him was extremely difficult to fight—but fight it she did. Instead, she smiled sweetly as both men walked out of Theatre.

'He seems quite taken with you, Annie,' the theatre sister remarked. 'I thought before it might have been because he was being polite but, no, I think he fancies you.'

Annie had no idea what to say so did the only thing that came to mind—she laughed. 'That's a good one.'

'I wish he'd fancy me,' the nurse grumbled.

'He wants *you* to show him around,' the theatre sister continued.

'It's protocol,' Annie argued, but laughed again. The only way she'd found to combat gossip was to treat it as though it were a joke. In this instance, the theatre sister wouldn't even begin to guess that Hayden had been purposely teasing her.

'Either way, dear, you'd better get going. Don't want Wesley covering for you again.'

'Right you are, Sister.' Annie didn't bother changing out

of her theatre greens and was waiting at the entrance to Theatres for Hayden. Wesley came out first, which surprised her.

'You seem to have bowled the new professor over with your supposed charm and girlish wit, but he respects me as a fellow doctor and colleague, rather than some bit of fluff on the side.' Wesley said his little spiel before stalking off, leaving Annie rather stunned at his words. She stared after her fellow registrar in surprise.

When she turned back around, it was to find Hayden standing in front of her.

'Wake up, Australia.'

'I'm awake. Let's go.' She walked him out of Theatres and down towards the ward. At the top of the ward she took the corridor to the right, which led to the surgical administration offices. 'You didn't need any help finding your way,' she noted as he walked smoothly alongside her.

'Correct.'

'So why?'

'I wanted to see how Wes would react.'

Annie smiled. 'You're such a tease, Hayden. And besides, he *loathes* being called Wes.'

'I thought as much but he doesn't have the guts to tell me. Have I just made matters worse for you?'

'No. I can handle him.'

'Good.' They'd reached Hayden's office and he beckoned her in, closing the door behind her. 'Honestly, the man is so attentive, I thought he was going to offer to shine my shoes.'

Annie laughed. 'That's Wesley.'

'I heard what he said to you.' Hayden said, all teasing gone.

'Hayden, I have six months left until I qualify. I don't have the luxury of worrying about other registrars and their personal gripes. So long as his work is up to standard, I don't care.'

'That's what I wanted to hear.'

'Another test passed?'

A slow smile spread across his lips. 'Yes.'

'Any more tests for today?'

'Who knows?' His grin increased.

'I'll take that as a no.' She stood, wanting to get out of there as fast as she could. Hayden, in this playful mood, only made her more nervous than usual. 'If there's nothing else, I'll get going.' When he didn't say anything, she turned on her heel and walked to the door.

'Annie.'

Her back was to him, her hand on the handle. 'Hmm?' She glanced over her shoulder.

'Want to have dinner and then shoot a few games of pool tonight?'

'I'd like to but I really have to study.'

'OK, then we won't make it a late night.'

Annie tilted her head to the side, wondering if he was teasing her or being sincere.

'Honest. Home by…nine? That gives you some time to study.'

She wanted to go. She wanted to spend time with him and she knew she'd get more study done *after* seeing him than if she declined his offer. She nodded firmly. 'Sure, but nine o'clock and not a minute later.'

'Chinese OK?'

'Great.'

'Meet me back here when you're through for the day.'

'It's a date.' The smile on her face was broad. Her eyes sparkled with delight and her entire body was zinging with the promise of time alone with Hayden. 'This is good,' she whispered excitedly. 'This is *very* good.'

CHAPTER FOUR

AFTER changing her clothes and doing a ward round, Annie stopped by Brenton's office and instead of Brenton found Natasha there.

'How are the kids?' she asked immediately.

'Hopefully, over the worst.'

'Glad to hear it.' She eyed her friend closely. 'How about you?'

'I'm OK.'

'Natasha.' Annie walked over and placed her hand on her friend's forehead. 'You're burning up.' She reached for the phone.

'Who are you calling?'

'Your husband.'

'I'm OK,' Natasha persisted.

'No, you're not, and you're not going to do anyone any good by being here.'

'Problem?' Hayden knocked on the open office door and walked in. 'I was just finishing up in A and E. What's wrong?'

'I have stubborn friends.'

Hayden felt Natasha's forehead. 'You must be Natasha, Brenton's wife.'

'Yes.' Natasha started to retch and Hayden quickly reached for the bin.

Annie spoke with Brenton and they arranged to get Natasha home. After she'd been sick, her temperature started to decrease. Annie quickly took care of the bin and returned to Brenton's office.

'A memorable first meeting,' Hayden mumbled as they shifted Natasha to the couch in the corner.

'Hey, she almost passed out the day I met her.' Annie's gaze met Hayden's and she smiled.

'How long until Brenton arrives?'

'Not long. They don't live far from the hospital. Brenton wanted me to arrange a replacement doctor.' Annie picked up the phone again and called the hospital switchboard, asking them to page another A and E doctor. When that was sorted, she returned to Natasha's side.

'Looks as though the worst is over. Her kids have all had this bug and Monty said it was a twenty-four-hour thing.' Annie shook her head. 'He shouldn't have let you come to work.' They stayed with Natasha until Brenton walked in.

'Tash!' He rushed to his wife's side, holding her close.

'Monty, give her some air.' Annie looked down at Natasha who was too lethargic to move.

'Tash? You OK, honey?'

'BJ,' Natasha muttered.

'She's too weak to move, Monty.'

'I'll get a wheelchair,' Hayden suggested.

'Thanks.' Brenton soothed his wife's forehead as Hayden left the room. As Natasha sat upright, she moaned.

'Are you going to be sick again?'

'She was sick?' Brenton was horrified.

'Yes. Uh…and you'll need to requisition a new bin,' Annie added with a nonchalant shrug.

'Here we go.' Hayden pushed a wheelchair in and Brenton assisted his wife into it.

'I'll take it from here. Annie, can you…?' He gestured to his office and started pushing the wheelchair out.

'Sure. I'll call you in the morning. Just go take care of her and the rest of your family.'

'Thanks, mate.' He disappeared, leaving Annie alone with Hayden again.

'Well, that was a bit of excitement,' she said with a sigh as she turned off the lights and headed for the door, making sure it was locked.

'You ready to leave?'

'Yes. I just need to get my bag.'

'Good. I'll lock my office and meet you back here in five.'

'Great.' She rushed off to her poky office and quickly packed her briefcase and bag before heading to the toilets. She quickly combed her riotous curls and applied some lip gloss. The black linen shorts and red cotton shirt she'd worn to work were fine to play pool in. 'Ready as I'll ever be.' She took a deep breath and headed towards Brenton's office.

He was there waiting and smiled when he saw her coming.

'Are we walking?' she asked as they headed out together.

'Yes. That's not a problem, is it?'

'The walking's not, the being seen leaving the hospital together, might be.' Annie tucked a curl behind her ear and glanced back at the hospital. There were plenty of people leaving at the moment and several had already seen her walk this far with him.

'People will gossip regardless.'

'Been there, done that?' she asked.

'Yes. You?'

'In spades.'

'Care to elaborate?'

She shrugged. 'I've had bad luck in relationships. When they end, they get gossiped about.' She glanced up at him. 'Probably shouldn't say anything more about it.'

'Why not?'

She laughed nervously. 'Because…' She took a deep breath and looked at him again. 'I *like* you and I don't want to scare you off.'

'We all have a past, Annie.'

'So you've been gossiped about, then?'

He was silent and for a moment she didn't think he'd answer. 'My divorce was a hot topic of conjecture for a while.'

'Did your wife work at the hospital?'

'*Ex*-wife and, no, she didn't but a few of her lovers did.'

'Ah.'

'I know how destroying the gossip can be. The way people suddenly stop talking when you walk into the room, the whispering as soon as you've gone down the corridor. But one thing I've learned is that I can't let hospital gossip rule my life.'

'I know but with regards to you and I, it's started already, Hayden, and you've only been at the hospital for one day. Theatre Sister is convinced you fancy me.' Hayden laughed and Annie wasn't sure whether to be flattered or upset. 'Is that funny?' They stopped at the pedestrian lights and she pushed the button with more force than was necessary.

He smiled down at her. 'I'm not laughing *at* you, Annie. I'm laughing in amazement and the fact that it's gone *that* far, *that* quickly.' He put his arm about her shoulders, his smile starting to fade and a serious light entering his eyes. 'I must say, though, that Theatre Sister is a very perceptive woman.'

It took a whole three seconds for his words to penetrate the fog surrounding Annie's brain. 'Oh!' The pedestrian light turned green and, taking her elbow, he ushered her across the street. Two doors down was the Chinese restaurant where he'd made reservations for their early dinner.

They enjoyed their dinner, talking quietly as they ate. Hayden didn't say anything more about their topic of conversation before they'd arrived at the restaurant and Annie didn't have the courage to broach it herself.

After eating, they headed to the pool hall. The instant she entered, she felt all anxiety and stress fall from her shoulders.

'Well, well, well,' Trevor said from behind the bar. 'Look who's walking in *together*! Is there a doctor in the house?'

'You crack me up.' Annie pretended to wipe tears from

her eyes while Trevor laughed at his own joke. 'Got a table free?'

'Number two is just waiting for you. Well, both of you, that is.'

'Great.'

'Drinks?'

'Usual for me, Trev.'

'I'll have what she's having,' Hayden replied, and headed to the back of the room towards table two. Annie followed and once they'd rid themselves of their bags and chosen their cues, Hayden leaned over and whispered, 'What's the usual?'

Annie grinned. 'Rocket Fuel cocktail.'

'What?'

She laughed. 'Lemonade. Your turn to break.' They played a game, Annie doing better than she had the other day.

'You really like it here, don't you?'

'Yes. I feel, free, alive and I can take all my frustrations out on sinking the balls and beating my opponent.'

'Really?' He sounded as though he didn't believe her. 'So you're going to beat me tonight?'

Annie lined up another shot, bent from the waist and leaning forward over the table. 'You've got that straight, mate. No more Ms Nice Guy. I'm going to wipe the floor wi—' A scream escaped her lips and she almost punctured the green felt with her cue as she felt something cool and smooth sliding up the inside of her leg.

She spun to glare at him as he quickly brought his cue back up beside him. 'Cheater.'

He looked around innocently. 'Who, me?'

Annie slowly advanced towards him. 'Yes…*you*.'

He skirted around the table but Annie continued to advance, trying to keep the annoyed look on her face when she really wanted to laugh.

'What did I do?'

'You know perfectly well. You ran the cue up my leg.'

She was close now. Too close! He'd stopped moving and they stood toe to toe.

'Lucky cue,' he breathed, before lowering his head. His lips briefly brushed hers.

Annie's eyelids fluttered closed. 'Mmm,' she moaned as she breathed in. The mild scent of his aftershave mixed with the warmth of his body was a heady combination. She lifted one hand and placed it tentatively on his arm. The feel of his firm biceps beneath her fingers only increased the excitement which was now coursing through her entire being.

Hayden pressed his lips to hers again before pulling back slightly to look down at her. She opened her eyes to gaze into his. He made no move to break the embrace and no move to increase it. The atmosphere between them thickened with every passing second, neither of them moving. It was as though they were trapped in some sort of time bubble, where there was only the two of them. Their minds, their souls and their hearts, all intertwined together. It was the most encompassing feeling Annie had ever experienced.

The sound of someone clearing their throat brought Annie back to earth with a thud.

She shifted backwards and was relieved when Hayden dropped his arms in a rather unhurried sort of manner. She couldn't believe she'd kissed Hayden. He was irresistible and with the taste of him still on her lips, it only made matters worse. She gave herself a little shake, bringing her head out of the clouds and back to reality.

'Sorry to interrupt,' Trevor said, a wide grin splitting his face.

'No problem,' Hayden remarked. 'We can always pick up where we left off.'

Trevor handed over the drinks and beat a hasty retreat. Annie took a sip of her drink and placed it on the table reserved for drinks which was against the wall. She couldn't believe she'd kissed Hayden, in the middle of the pool hall, for anyone to see. Thank goodness none of the hospital staff came here. She glanced at Hayden to find him watching her. She smiled shyly and licked her lips, tasting not only the sweetness of the lemonade but the desire she felt for her boss.

They gazed at each other for a few more moments before Annie whispered, 'Say something.'

His lips twitched into a slow smile. 'It's still your turn.'

To do what? To have another drink? To kiss him again? Her heart rate, which had just started to settle down a little, picked up pace at the thought. 'Hmm?'

'It's your turn.' He pointed to the table.

'Oh. Yeah. Right.' She forced her legs to work and headed back to the table. If she didn't clear her head, he would most definitely win. So, he wanted to mess with her concentration, eh? Well, two could play at that game. She leaned over the table in a provocative way, her shirt edging open to reveal a tantalising hint of cleavage.

Annie was directly opposite him and dared a peek at him from beneath her lashes. A sense of feminine satisfaction coursed through her when she saw his Adam's apple working overtime as he swallowed.

She potted a ball.

'So now that you've kissed me,' she purred as she prowled around the table, 'I guess we'll be getting married soon.'

He'd just taken a sip of his drink, and at her words spurted it out of his mouth over the floor.

'Real classy.'

'Did you say *married*?'

'Yes. Is there a problem, darling?' She made sure her tone had the right amount of innocence and looked up at him with concern.

Hayden stared at her for a long moment before shaking his head. 'Stop teasing, Annie.'

'Who's teasing?'

'You *want* to get married?'

'Sure. I'll be forty in just over two weeks' time and my biological clock is ticking.'

'So you're out husband-hunting?'

'I wouldn't put it like that exactly. I'm out there, swimming around in the sea, seeing if there are any compatible fishes.'

'Why? Why are you compelled to do this?'

Annie frowned, all pretence gone. 'Why? Because it's what I've wanted all my life.' She took a breath and plunged on. 'Don't you want to get married again?'

'No.' The way he said the word clearly brooked no argument.

'You're going to let one bad experience ruin the possibility of lifelong happiness?'

Hayden walked to the table and slammed the cue into the white ball, which in turn cracked loudly against another ball before the second ball rolled into a pocket. Annie let go the fact that it wasn't even his turn.

'I've had several bad experiences.'

'Then learn from them.'

She was taken aback at his tone. It was harsh and callous. As he continued to pot every ball on the table, she watched him with a mixture of compassion and bewilderment. When he'd finished, he threw the cue onto the table, gripped the edge with both hands and leaned across, his gaze never leaving hers.

'My marriage was a nightmare. My ex-wife was unfaithful time and time again. She hurt me in ways I never dreamed possible.'

'But not all women are like that,' Annie felt compelled to point out, but he just shook his head and turned away. She came around the table and stood next to him, their backs to the rest of the room. 'To never risk loving or trusting again... Hayden, it will break you in the end. Marriages *can* and *do* work out. Not all of them are bad.'

'Did your parents have a happy marriage?'

'No, and, look, I'm still willing to try it…because I'm not them!' She paused. 'What about your folks?'

'Still together after forty-three years.'

'There you go, then. Proof that it does work.'

'Sure…but I'm not them.' He turned and grabbed his briefcase and although his mimicking of her words had bruised a little, Annie followed suit. It wasn't the way she'd envisaged the evening turning out but at least she was getting to know him. Right? She was digging a little deeper beneath the surface and really finding out who this man was.

Annie waved goodnight to Trevor and together she and Hayden walked out into the street. Neither of them spoke for a while but she knew she couldn't let it lie. He'd said some pretty important things and if she didn't push any further now, she might regret it later.

She was attracted to him and she needed to decide whether to take that attraction to the next level or to back off while her heart was still in one piece. They stopped at a red light and waited.

'So you don't want to get married again.'

'No.'

'What about children? Don't you want children?'

'No.'

'How can you say that?' she demanded. 'Do you have nieces or nephews?'

'Yes.'

'And aren't they gorgeous?'

'Yes…but I can give them back.' She was starting to dig too deep. She was pushing him, and the more she did, the more he wanted to back right off. He might be attracted to her but he wasn't going to let her size him up as husband and father material. The light turned green and he headed off, checking to make sure she was still beside him. Regardless of how he was feeling right now, he didn't want Annie storming off in a huff by herself. It simply wasn't safe.

Another glance, though, revealed she was far from huffy. A puzzled and concerned frown creased her forehead and he started to feel like a first-class swine for his attitude. She wasn't to know what had happened in his past, how Lonnie had ruined not only their marriage but his hope and trust as well.

They were nearing their apartment block and when they got to the stairwell he held the door for her, just as he'd done earlier that morning when they'd come back from their run. Man! That seemed like a lifetime ago.

As they mounted the stairs, he could feel more questions brewing in that intelligent mind of hers. His temper had cooled somewhat and even though he was attracted to his petite next-door neighbour, there was still a line which he'd firmly drawn and which no one crossed.

'You're serious?' she queried as they stood outside their apartment doors. 'You honestly don't want to get married?'

'Correct.'

'OK. *That* part I can comprehend, but the children?' She looked at him, her brown eyes boring directly into his soul. 'You would make such a wonderful father, Hayden. Look at the way you bandaged my knee this morning.'

'I'm a doctor, Annie.'

'Or the way you handled Wesley.'

'I'm used to dealing with staff.'

She tilted her head and smiled at him. There was nothing coy or insincere about it, neither was there pity. It was genuine. 'You'd be wonderful with children,' she said softly, her heart in her words.

Hayden felt a twisting in his gut and wondered how things had escalated so fast without him realising. It was Annie. She'd bowled him over from their first meeting three days ago and she was continuing to do so. Never before had a woman got beneath his skin so quickly, and that in itself should breed caution.

'I know.' The words were all but choked out of him. 'My daughter, Liana, died when she was four weeks old.'

He clenched his jaw tight, ignoring Annie's gasp of horror and determined to squash the emotions that never failed to move him. The mental picture of his baby girl floated to the forefront of his mind and he closed his eyes momentarily, fighting desperately for control.

He felt Annie's fingers against his arm and he shifted quickly, burnt by her tender touch. He dragged in a deep breath and opened his eyes. Annie's own had filled with tears and her fingers now covered her mouth in shock.

'Oh, Hayden,' she whispered.

'Out of my mockery of a marriage came the most precious gift I could ever receive, and then that, too, was taken away from me.' He shook his head and unlocked his door. She wanted to go to him, to comfort him, to get him to open up some more and talk things out. She felt closer to him right this very second than she had to any other man in her life.

He was different.

He was special.

And right now he had a right to his privacy.

She dug in her bag for her own keys. After she'd found them, she crossed to his side and, standing on tiptoe, pressed her lips to his cheek. 'I'm sorry for pushing.'

'Really?'

'You sound as though you don't believe me.'

He looked down at the floor and Annie stepped back. 'You weren't to know.'

'Now that I do, I'll endeavour to be a little more…tactful.'

He raised his eyebrows, indicating he didn't think it would be possible, and Annie smiled, glad to be back on more even ground.

'See you tomorrow,' she whispered, and together they opened their doors and went their separate ways.

Hayden managed to avoid any one-on-one time with Annie for the next two days. It helped, being the boss and the person who drew up the rosters for the staff. He had changed the roster first thing Tuesday morning, with Annie doing a double shift on Tuesday and then being on call for Wednesday night. If she had a problem with it, she didn't say so.

On Thursday morning, he was closing his apartment door when he heard the door to the stairwell open and an ashen-faced Annie come through it. She looked awful. He rushed to her side, slipping one arm about her waist to support her. The fact that she didn't protest told him she wasn't well.

'Give me your key,' he demanded, and she handed it over.

'It's OK.'

'It's not OK.' He held her close while opening her door. She sagged against him even more, and without another thought he scooped her up into his arms and carried her over the threshold. She rested her head against his chest, breathing in the glorious scent of him.

'Mmm.' She closed her eyes. It felt wonderful to be off her feet. All night long she'd been fine but then about an hour ago all her energy had disappeared, as though it had been drained from her body. 'I tried to take a taxi home,' she told him. 'but there weren't any.'

He carried her through to the bedroom and knelt down to place her on the futon. 'Why didn't you hire a bed as well?' Hayden mumbled, feeling her forehead. 'You're burning up, Annie. Have you taken anything?' When he received no reply, he stroked a finger down her cheek. 'Annie? Wake up. Have you taken anything?'

'No,' came the muffled reply.

He rummaged around in her kitchen until he found the first-aid box and took her some paracetamol and a glass of water. 'This will help,' he said as she swallowed them down. He turned on the air-conditioning and collected a cloth and a bowl of water to sponge her down. She was wearing a light patterned singlet top and a pair of red shorts—the graze on her knee was healing over nicely. The brevity of her clothes would make it easier for him to sponge her.

He searched in her laundry for a bucket but couldn't find one. 'I'm just going next door,' he told her, not sure whether she could hear him. He quickly found a bucket in his apartment and returned, all the while praying she wouldn't vomit in his absence.

Thankfully, she was still lying lethargically on the bed where he'd left her, and he returned to her side. He felt like a first-class heel for changing the roster, especially as his motive had been to put distance between them. Perhaps if she hadn't had to do that double shift on Tuesday, she might have been able to fight off the virus which was going around.

He knelt down and sat on the futon next to her, dabbing the wet cloth against her forehead, then her cheeks. He wiped her neck, shoulders and arms before lifting her top to wipe her abdomen. He kept rinsing the cloth and wiping her down again and again, willing her temperature to drop.

As he pushed her curls back from her face with his fingertips, wiping her forehead down with the cloth, he was struck by her beauty. It was wholesome, not conventional. Lonnie had been the other way around and he knew for a fact that wholesome beauty, the kind that came from within, was the kind that mattered the most. Annie was open, honest and giving. That much he'd picked up during their short but involving acquaintance.

No. They were more than acquaintances who happened to live next door to each other. Since last Friday he'd come to learn a lot about Annie and most of it had surprised him. There was still a lot more he wanted to know, her previous relationship with Adam currently top of the list, but he could wait…at least until she'd recovered from this virus.

He kept sponging her down and when he checked the clock he was surprised to find it was almost eight-thirty. He reached into his trouser pocket for his mobile phone and called the hospital. He spoke to his secretary, telling her he'd been unavoidably detained, and then asked to be transferred to Brenton's office.

'Dr Worthington.'

'Brenton, it's Hayden. Annie's come down with this virus.'

'Are you with her?'

'Yes. Her fever hasn't broken and I don't want her left alone until it does.'

'Understandable. Tash has just started her shift and no doubt you have the same heads of department meeting this morning that I have.'

'Correct. I wasn't sure who to call. I don't even know if Annie has siblings or parents or what.'

'Her parents wouldn't come and she's an only child. Listen, the first meeting this morning isn't important so if you can stay with her for the next hour or so I'll see what I can do about getting Tash to come around about eleven-ish.'

'Right. Pass on my apologies to the meeting.'

'Will do—and, Hayden, I'm glad you're with her. Annie had a bad year last year and needs a lot of support.'

'Keep in contact,' Hayden said, before disconnecting the call. He looked down at Annie for a second before checking her temperature. It was slowly coming down. He started his sponging circuit again, his mind mulling over what Brenton had said. Why wouldn't her parents come? He supposed, with the way his own family rallied around to support one another, it was a foreign concept to him when other people's families didn't do the same.

And she was an only child. Another interesting bit of information. Although he'd often felt burdened with his sisters, he wouldn't want to be without them. Was that one of the reasons why Annie seemed to want children?

Annie groaned and clutched her stomach. Hayden felt her forehead once more and realised her temperature had gone up again. She sat up and he held the bucket while she was sick, soothing her with calming words.

After that, she slowly began to pick up. Her temperature dropped and she settled into a more natural sleep. Hayden pulled the cotton sheet over her and lay down on top of the covers beside her. He closed his eyes while listening to her breathing, glad it was deep and even. Hopefully now she could sleep the rest of the virus off.

The phone he held in his hand buzzed and he sat up, momentarily disorientated. He pressed the button to connect the call.

'Professor Robinson.' He glanced at his watch as he spoke. *Ten o'clock!*

'Hayden? It's Natasha. I was just ringing to see how Annie is.'

He glanced across at Annie. She was still sleeping. He levered himself up from the futon, surprised he'd fallen asleep. Then again, he hadn't been sleeping all that well lately.

'Hayden?'

'Sorry. She's fine.' He reached down and placed his hand on Annie's forehead. 'Temperature feels quite normal.' She began to stir and he quickly left the room so he didn't wake her.

'Has she been sick?'

'Yes, just over an hour ago. She's been sleeping since then.'

'Good. That means she's over the worst, but what about you?'

'I had this bug two weeks ago.'

'In Perth?'

'Yes.'

'You didn't bring it over here with you, did you?'

'Hey, now. As I understand it, your children came down with the virus before I'd even met you.'

Natasha laughed. 'Good point. Thanks for staying with Annie this morning. Brenton's managed to fiddle the roster and organise a replacement for me, so I'll head on over now. Helps, being married to the head of department.'

'I'm sure Annie appreciates it.'

'It's the least we can do for her. I'll see you soon.'

Hayden disconnected the call but didn't move. It was comforting to know Annie had friends who would do this sort of thing for her, especially with her serious lack of family.

'Hey.'

Hayden spun around to see Annie standing in the doorway of her bedroom. 'What are you doing up? Get back to bed.' He crossed quickly to her side as he spoke and placed his arm around her shoulders.

'I just need to visit the little girls' room,' she protested with a laugh. That stopped him.

'Uh… OK.'

'Gee, thanks.' She chuckled weakly as she shuffled off towards the bathroom.

Once there, she steadied herself against the wall, waiting for the room to stop spinning before she moved again. She knew if she took too long, Hayden would get worried and no doubt insist upon helping her, which was taking his knight in shining armour routine way too far. She tried to move quickly but found it impossible.

'Annie?' He knocked on the door a few minutes later.

'I'm fine. I just want to brush my teeth.'

Hayden waited for her and then helped her back into her bed. He smoothed the hair back from her forehead and checked her temperature again. 'You're over the worst.'

'That's your official verdict, Doctor?'

He smiled. 'Yes.' Hayden gazed into her eyes, giving in to the impulse to drown in the brown, chocolaty depths. Whenever he looked at her, his resolve seemed to crumble. After their discussion on Monday night, he'd decided to be just a friendly but aloof neighbour and boss, yet here he was, in her apartment, crouched on her futon, gazing deeply into her eyes. The scary thing was, he felt a warm and calming sensation in the pit of his stomach. He brushed a curl from her forehead and caressed her cheek with the backs of his fingers. 'You're beautiful, Annie Beresford.'

Annie wanted to look away but found herself mesmerised by him. It was nice of him to say such nice things, even though she knew it wasn't the truth.

'You don't believe me,' he stated, nodding slightly. 'I don't lie.' He bent his head and brushed his lips across hers.

Annie pulled back. 'Don't.'

Hayden stared at her, surprised.

'I don't want you to get what I've got.'

He smiled with understanding and brushed her lips once more, glad this time she didn't pull away. 'News flash, Dr Beresford. If I were going to catch it from you, I would have already been infected by now.'

'Oh.' She glanced up at him, knowing what she was about to do was a mistake but nevertheless needing to do it. 'In that case…' She reached out and slid her fingers into the softness of his hair. 'Give me this special treatment…' she urged his head closer '…you've prescribed.'

His smile increased. 'You *are* feeling better,' he murmured against her lips, before pressing his to her own. He'd told himself a few days ago that whatever he was feeling towards Annie was going to stop—yet here he was, unable to resist her.

He groaned against her mouth, knowing his self-control was almost about to snap.

Annie sighed into the sweet and gentle torture he was inflicting upon her. It was the most mind-drugging sensation she'd ever experienced. She felt as though she were floating through the air surrounded by the sensual daze that was Hayden Robinson.

When he pulled back, Annie sighed, relaxing into the pillows even further. Reluctantly, she opened her eyelids which felt as though they weighed a ton. 'Thank you for looking after me.'

Hayden nodded. 'Do you remember much?'

'No.' She closed her eyes but smiled. 'Sorry.'

'Sleep, Annie.' His tender fingers soothed across her forehead and down her cheek. 'I have to go to the hospital now but Natasha's coming to take over.'

'Mmm.'

Her breathing had evened out again and, unable to stop himself, he brushed one last kiss against her lips. And that *is* the last one, he told himself sternly. Just because she was sick, it was no reason for him to give in to these erratic impulses, especially when he knew it was the wrong thing to do. Annie was charming, honest and a breath of fresh air, but she also wanted things in life he wasn't prepared to give.

CHAPTER FIVE

WHEN Annie woke the next time, it was to find the afternoon sun peaking in from behind her closed curtains and her stomach growling with hunger. She frowned, wondering why she was in bed in the afternoon. She lifted the cotton sheet off her, surprised to find she was dressed in clothes, rather than her PJs.

Her answer came when she tried to get out of bed, amazed that every muscle in her body ached. She remembered she'd been ill.

'Annie?' Natasha walked into the room. 'So finally you're awake. Nice to have you back.'

Annie's frown continued as she stared at Natasha. For some reason she'd thought Hayden was here.

'How are you feeling?'

'Terrible.'

Natasha nodded. 'Every muscle aches?'

'Yes.'

'Good. You're in third-stage recovery. You'll feel a lot better tomorrow.'

'I hope so.' Annie managed to sit up. 'I thought… Hayden was here.'

'He was. He left just before eleven o'clock when I arrived. He nursed you through the worst parts.'

Annie gasped and covered her face with her hands. 'I was sick,' she groaned. 'I can't believe he saw me vomit.'

'So? He's a doctor, Annie. He saw me do it the other night.'

'Yeah, but you're not interested in him.'

'Ah…so you *are* interested?'

'Yes, but it won't work.'

'Why not?' Natasha sat down on the futon, crossing her legs beneath her.

'Comfortable?'

'Yes. Come on, why wouldn't it work between you and Hayden?'

'I want marriage and a family.' Annie shrugged as though it were that simple.

'So?'

'And he doesn't.'

'Are you sure about this?'

'Yes.' It was not her place to speak about his baby nor what he'd shared regarding his marriage. Although she was curious to learn more, she only wanted to know what Hayden wanted to share.

'So? Change his mind.'

'Oh, just like that?'

Natasha smiled. 'You're a woman, aren't you? Use the weapons at your disposal.'

Annie laughed then winced in pain. 'You're nuts. Is that what you did to Monty?'

'He and I were a different story.'

'Ah, so you don't practise what you preach.'

'Come on, Annie. Hayden is obviously interested in you so why not try and get him interested in a permanent relationship?'

'What if it doesn't work? I can't handle heartbreak any more. Adam was the last straw.'

'But Adam was wrong for you.'

'Oh, *now* you tell me.'

'You know what I mean. He's wasn't…caring enough. Hayden has proved himself this morning to be extremely caring, not only for your health but your well-being as well.'

'What do you mean?'

'He's called me every half-hour for progress reports.'

'Really?'

'Yes.'

'But he's a doctor.' Annie squashed the feelings of joy.

'True, but it wasn't the usual doctor-patient follow-up call. Every half-hour, Annie.'

'Really?' she asked again, unable to believe it.

'Would I lie to you?'

'No.'

'He cancelled his morning's schedule to stay here with you.'

'Only because there was no one else available,' Annie rationalised. 'Both you and Monty would have been at the hospital.'

'Still, Annie, he stayed. That says a lot to me.'

'Every man I get interested in seems so right for me in the beginning. Then I dig a little deeper, commit myself a little further, and end up getting hurt. Why can't I find a man who likes me for who I am deep down inside, warts and all, and who wants to settle down and have a couple of kids? Why doesn't that man exist?' Annie's voice broke off in a sob and Natasha instantly enveloped her in a hug.

'You really like Hayden, don't you?' her friend whispered.

'Yes.'

'It's true that you've picked bad apples in the past, Annie, and you've been hurt. But they weren't right for you. If you'd gone through with marrying any of them, you'd now be going through a bitter divorce and, more than likely, have a few children attached.'

'Is this supposed to make me feel better?'

Natasha smiled. 'I'm just trying to point out marrying the wrong person can be a nightmare.'

'So Hayden tells me.' Her tone was glum with a healthy dose of dejection. 'I shouldn't get my hopes up about him. I need to protect myself.' She blew her nose and tossed the tissue at the bin—she missed. 'He kissed me. So what? It was just a kiss.' She almost believed her nonchalant tone and ignored the little voice which told her she was fooling nobody.

'A kiss between friends.' Natasha nodded, pacifying her.

'Exactly.'

'It didn't mean anything.'

'Exac— No. I think it *did* mean something but I'm not going to delve any deeper into it than I already have. Sure, there's an attraction between us but it isn't enough, Tash, and I have to face that fact.'

'OK, then.'

Annie's stomach growled. 'Any chance of the patient getting something to eat?'

'Of course.' Natasha scrambled off the futon. 'Stay there. I'll bring it to you.' Just as Natasha reached the door, the phone started ringing. 'Right on time.' She disappeared but came back a moment later, holding the ringing phone out to Annie. 'I believe it's for you.'

Annie quickly connected the call. 'Hello?'

'Annie? You're awake.'

'Yes.'

'How do you feel?'

'Sore.'

Hayden chuckled and the deep sound washed over her, warming her all the way to her toes. 'I'm not surprised. Listen, don't worry about your on-call shift tonight. I've changed the roster so you now have until Sunday afternoon off.'

'Thanks, but I'll probably be fine by tomorrow evening.' If she wasn't at work, she'd have more time to think, and right now thinking was the last thing she wanted to do because, regardless of where her thoughts started out, they invariably led to Hayden.

'Still, I think it's better if you rest and recuperate completely before coming back to work.'

She closed her eyes in agony. 'Well, I guess I'll take a few days off, then. Thanks.'

'I'd better go. I'll drop by after work.'

'Thanks, Hayden, but there's really no need. I'm feeling much better now.' She grimaced, realising how ungrateful her words sounded. 'But if you want to…' She trailed off, knowing she was digging herself in deeper.

'I'll see you then.'

She held onto the receiver for a moment after he'd hung up, wondering how on earth things had escalated so quickly. Hayden would drop around tonight. She wondered if Natasha would stay and be the go-between? No. When Hayden arrived, she needed to be alone with him. She needed to say there could be no more kisses, no more gentle caresses and no more melting smiles. She needed to preserve her heart as best she could because she was beginning to fear that with Hayden Robinson she was in danger of giving it to him on a silver platter.

This is what I need to do. I need to ask her, get her to agree and let her know that I'm not really using her. That's not my intention. Hayden stood outside Annie's apartment door and straightened his tie.

She's going to smile at you and you're going to weaken but you are *not* going to kiss her. That's got nothing to do with it. You need a date for a family function and that's all this is about.

Hayden raised his hand and knocked on her door and held out a bunch of brightly coloured gerberas when she opened it.

'Thought these might cheer you up,' he stated as she stepped back to allow him to enter. 'My sisters love them and, because they have no perfume, they're not likely to upset your sensitive stomach.'

Annie was touched. Why did he have to be so…so…nice?

She couldn't remember the last time a man had brought her flowers. Especially one she wasn't even dating. She and Hayden had to be just friends. Nothing more. Although the attraction was there and they appeared to have quite a bit in common, they wanted different things out of life. At least, that's what she'd been telling herself since his earlier phone call.

She'd been going over and over in her head the words she wanted to say to him. Practising and rehearsing until she was positive they were perfect. Now all her good intentions had blown out the door the instant she'd seen him standing there. The flowers hadn't helped her resolve one little bit. Still…she was touched by his thoughtfulness.

Annie sighed and looked at him, then back to the flowers cradled in her arms. 'Thank you,' she whispered, her gaze meeting his once more. 'They're lovely.'

'I'm glad you like them.'

He seemed genuinely pleased that he'd been able to please her. Oh, he would be such an easy man to fall in love with.

Annie realised she was gazing up at him like he'd given her the world, and abruptly turned away, forcing her wobbly legs to take her to the kitchen. 'Let me see if I can find a vase or something to put them in. I hadn't planned on receiving flowers so soon after moving.' She was babbling but didn't seem able to stop. 'Well, if I can't find one, I'm sure I can borrow one from Natasha although what to do with them in the meantime may be a bit of a problem.' She'd been opening and closing cupboard doors as she spoke, searching for a vase.

Hayden put his arm on her shoulder and gently turned her to face him. 'Annie?' He looked at her, a puzzled frown creasing his forehead. 'They're just flowers.'

'Uh… I…know,' she faltered, feeling even more foolish. She put the gerberas in the sink and filled it with some water. 'Would you like a drink?'

'No. I'd like you to sit down. You're recuperating, remember?' With his hand still on her shoulder, he guided her to the sofa. After she was off her feet he removed his hand, but that didn't stop the churning that was going on inside her already queasy stomach. 'You're not looking too good.' He went to place his hand on her forehead but she pulled back, not wanting him to touch her again. She was already reeling from too many unwanted sensations.

'I'm fine. Natasha wouldn't have left otherwise.'

'I thought she might have waited until I arrived.'

'So she could hand over? I'm not completely helpless, Hayden.' Her words came out clipped and she instantly regretted them. She couldn't help that the man sent her insides spiralling with one simple touch. Or the fact that his innocent gesture of the flowers had the ability to touch her so deeply.

'I wasn't suggesting you were.' He eyed her critically before nodding. 'You're an impatient patient.'

'So?'

'So am I. I hate being sick, which is why I thought the flowers might help cheer you up.'

Annie closed her eyes momentarily. 'They did.' You need to get your mind back on track, she reminded herself sternly, but it was easier to practise in the mirror what she wanted to say than do it in person with Hayden. She opened her eyes to find him watching her intently.

'So how was the hospital today? I hope the meetings you missed on account of me this morning weren't too important.'

He shrugged. 'It's fine. Meetings are meetings, Annie. You were sick.'

'Well, I appreciate you staying with me.'

'You've obviously had a shower and changed.' He pointed to her outfit of comfortable three-quarter-length trousers and baggy T-shirt. 'I hope Natasha was here to help you.'

'Yes. I may be a bad patient but I'm not completely stupid.'

He smiled at her. 'Glad to hear it. The last thing you needed was to keel over in the shower due to lack of energy.'

'I'm fine.'

He sat forward in his chair and she wondered if he, too,

had picked up on the strained atmosphere between them. Something wasn't right and as far as Annie was concerned it had everything to do with those kisses he'd placed on her lips before he'd left this morning.

'Hayden—'

'Annie—'

They spoke at the same time and then laughed, the tension easing slightly. 'You go first,' she offered, chickening out.

He stood, feeling uncharacteristically uncomfortable. What was wrong with him? He'd asked women out before—even just as friends—so why was he so anxious about asking Annie out? 'Are you free two weeks on Saturday?'

'Pardon?'

He'd completely surprised her. 'I've checked the current roster and have made sure Wesley's on duty so we're both free, but you may have other plans for that day.'

It was her birthday two weeks on Saturday. 'Why?'

'My sister is getting married and I was wondering if you'd like to come to the wedding with me.'

Annie stared at him in disbelief 'Married?'

'Yes. Came as a bit of a shock to me as well as she's only known the guy for three months, but there it is.' He scowled. 'Didn't even tell me she was engaged, but that's Rowena for you. Impulsive.'

Annie was a little confused. 'Why do you want me to go with you?'

'Because if I go alone, I'll have all three of my sisters, and probably my mother, trying to match me up with any unattached females in the room. All three of them want to see me in a relationship again and, quite frankly, it can get a little overbearing at times.'

She smiled. 'You're scared of your sisters.' She nodded at his appalled expression. 'I can't believe it. The great orthopaedic surgeon Hayden Robinson is scared of his little sisters and his mummy! Well, I never.'

'That's not it at all. It's just that it's not worth the head-ache or the bother. At Brigeeta's wedding I was married to Lonnie and everyone was whispering about my lack of judgement in choosing a suitable wife.'

'Sounds ominous. I take it your family didn't like her?'

'No, and my sisters, in particular, never hid that fact. They were polite to her, of course, and did everything they could to accept her into the family, but to be fair to them Lonnie made no effort.'

'Perhaps that's why they didn't like her,' Annie ventured.

'Perhaps. At Katrina's wedding, I was newly divorced and had every female member of my family either trying to match me up or feeling sorry for me. Great-aunts and grandmothers included. At this point in my life, I—'

'You don't want to go through that again?'

'No, I don't.'

'And that's why you're asking me,' she stated.

'Yes. Are you free?'

'As a matter of fact, I am.'

'You'll do it?'

'Why me?'

'Because we're friends.'

'Come on, Hayden. If you take me home to meet Mum and Dad, they're going to think a lot more is going on between us. It's your sister's wedding!' He looked down at the carpet for a moment and then back to Annie. It was then that things clicked in to place. 'You *want* them to think there's more going on between us, don't you?' She nodded to herself. 'That way, they'll get off your back and won't bother with the matchmaking routine.'

'Yes.'

'So…' Annie leaned back into the cushions and crossed her arms over her chest, eyeing him carefully. 'Are we supposed to act the happy couple?'

He smiled at her and her insides melted into a pool of mush. Did he have any idea the way he affected her with just one look? He raised his eyebrows and she realised he did.

'I see.'

'It won't be that hard, Annie. We're already attracted to each other.'

She shook her head at his arrogance. 'I suppose it will give you the perfect opportunity to kiss me any time you like.'

'This plan definitely has good incentives.'

'What if I don't *want* you to kiss me?'

Hayden crossed to her side and sat down beside her. He was close and the scent of him—freshly laundered shirt, aftershave and hospital aroma, all mingled together—created a heady combination. One that wove around her senses, driving her closer to distraction.

'Is that true?' Hayden's breath fanned her cheek and she worked harder to resist him. He brushed a few curls away from her face before cupping her chin and bringing it closer to his own. 'We have a chemistry between us, Annie, that neither of us can truly deny.' His words caressed her and she closed her eyes, waiting with seething impatience for his lips to meet hers.

'You feel it.' He kissed one cheek. 'I feel it.' He kissed her other cheek. 'Sometimes,' he whispered against her mouth, 'I'm powerless to fight it. Like now.'

It wasn't until his lips were pressed firmly against hers that she realised she'd been holding her breath. Annie sighed into the kiss, melting into him as his arm came around her waist, urging her closer. A raging fever burned her entire body and it had nothing to do with the virus. How could this be so…so…encompassing? All rational thought left her as she focused solely on the emotions Hayden's touch evoked.

Annie couldn't get enough of him. He was like a drug and she was finally allowed to have her fix. She didn't care that the craving wouldn't go away, only that she could now have her fill of him.

'Mmm,' he groaned as he hauled her across and onto his lap without breaking contact. He plundered her mouth, wanting to know and feel her innermost secrets. She fitted perfectly into his arms, her warm body pressed firmly against his own, sending one shock wave after another through him.

Up until now, up until this very moment, the kisses they'd shared had been merely appetisers. This…this was leading onto the main course and she was every bit as delicious as he'd fantasised. For hours he'd lain awake, wanting to kiss her gorgeous mouth in exactly this way. Now that he was actually in the middle of the experience, it was surpassing his dreams as she leaned into him, matching his enthusiasm.

The thrumming reverberating in her ears was an echo of her fiercely pounding heartbeat and for a moment she knew instinctively that his heart was pounding the same, intense rhythm. It was as though they had been made for each other because never in her entire thirty-nine years, forty-nine weeks and five days had she *ever* felt this way when a man had kissed her.

They both pulled back at the same time, gasping desperately for air. She gazed into his desire-filled blue eyes, knowing he was seeing the exact same emotion in her brown ones. After gulping in a breath, he urged her lips to his and there was no way she was going to argue.

The onslaught continued, taking them both to new heights. A fire that started in one spread quickly to the other, neither wanting the flames to be doused, but fanned instead. Annie started trembling and Hayden's hold on her increased.

'Annie,' he breathed a moment or two later as he pressed tender kisses across her cheek and down her neck.

'I know,' she murmured, understanding completely what he was saying. The emotions they were both feeling were far too intense for words. She tilted her head to allow him better access to her neck, the small kisses continuing to fuel the fire within. 'Oh, Hayden. This is… I don't know *what* it is.'

He groaned again, memorising the taste of her skin on his lips. It was like the sweetest nectar in the world and one which was highly addictive. He could get used to kissing Annie Beresford on a regular basis. That thought alone was enough to jump-start his sluggish brain.

'You'll definitely have to marry me,' she whispered near his ear as her teeth nipped lightly at his ear lobe.

'What?' Ignoring the goose-bumps which had just rippled down his neck, Hayden pushed her upright. He stared at her as though she had two heads. He cleared his throat, trying to calm the overwhelming urge to bolt. 'This is another one of your jokes, right?'

From somewhere she found the strength to move off his lap and sit beside him again. 'What makes you think that? I do like you, Hayden—*a lot*. We may be compatible, mentally and physically, but emotionally we want different things out of life. I want to get married. I want to have children.'

'To just anyone?'

'No. If I'd wanted to marry just anyone, I'd have done so by now. No. I want the perfect man for me. My soul mate.'

'Soul mates are a waste of time.'

'Really? Have you asked your parents that?'

'What do you know about my parents? You know nothing about them.'

Annie didn't take offence at his words and surprised him by smiling and cupping his cheek with her hand. There was nothing condescending or patronising in her touch, just tenderness. 'They raised you to be the caring and thoughtful man you are.' She paused and withdrew her hand.

Hayden worked hard not to drag it back to his face. He *wanted* her to touch him. He *wanted* her to delve into his psyche and tell him everything was going to be all right but he was a big boy now and he knew that life didn't always turn out the way you planned.

'Listen, Hayden, all I'm saying is that you can't kiss me with such overwhelming passion, holding nothing back and taking me to the spiralling heights of wonderment, just for *fun*! It messes with my heart and my mind.'

Her words were said with a hint of self-preservation and that alone was enough to bring him back to reality with a thump. Hayden raked his fingers through his hair and stood. 'Look, Annie, I didn't mean for things to get out of hand. I was just trying to show that—'

'I know what you were trying to show, Hayden, and I agree that things got a little out of control. In light of that and your sudden desire to escape as fast as you can, I suggest we don't repeat the performance.'

'Annie, you're blowing this way out of proport—'

She held up her hand to silence him and forced her body to respond to the signals her brain was sending. Slowly, she stood to face him. 'You may think I'm being ultra-female and blowing this out of proportion, but that's only according to your male sensibilities. You were right when you said we had a natural chemistry between us. We do, Hayden, but we both want completely different things out of life.' She closed her eyes and looked down at the floor for a moment before meeting his gaze once more. 'So, when we go to your sister's wedding—no kissing. You of all people should know about self-preservation.'

He stared at her, listening to what she was saying but unable to believe he was hearing it. She was truly like no other woman he'd ever met, and that *included* his sisters. Never had he met a woman who would rationalise her emotions so logically—probably the doctor in her. He appreciated her honesty.

'Hayden?'

'Yes.' He took a step towards the door. 'You're right, Annie. I do know about self-preservation. I also know it isn't my intention to break your heart.'

'I know.'

She smiled at him so sweetly, so knowledgeably that the urge to haul her into his arms and kiss her again almost overpowered him. Almost…

'I need to go.' It was a statement and one she didn't refute. Instead, she calmly walked him to the door.

'Thanks for looking after me, today—oh, and for the flowers.'

Hayden nodded and was glad when the door to her apartment closed with him on the other side. He quickly went to his own apartment, trying to figure out why the wall he'd built around his heart so many years ago felt as though it was starting to crumble.

'You're not going there again.' His words were stern and after collecting his briefcase where he'd left it just before he'd stopped by Annie's apartment, he walked to his desk and sat down to do some work.

It took a few minutes but thankfully his brain was willing to co-operate by pigeonholing all thoughts of Annie into a nice little compartment so he could concentrate on his work. Almost an hour later, the phone rang.

'Professor Robinson,' he answered.

'Hayd.'

There was only one person who called him that disgusting abbreviation of his name and that was Adam. 'Hi, Adam.'

'Sorry it's taken me a few days to get back to you, cous.'

'No problem. So how are things?'

'Not bad, not bad at all. I started a new job a few months back and things are starting to look up.'

'Are you still in the Geelong area?'

'Ah, no. I'm around the coast in East Gippsland.'

Hayden frowned. 'What on earth are you doing there?' They discussed Adam's new job and the property he was thinking of buying. They discussed the weather, the family and Hayden's professorship.

'You know I'm working at Geelong General hospital?'

'Really? I thought you were based in Melbourne.'

'No. Geelong.' Hayden waited, hoping Adam might mention that he knew someone who worked there—namely Annie—but he didn't.

'Like it?'

'Yeah. It's quite good. The staff I'm working with are really great, especially my registrars.' Come on, Adam. Mention her.

'What do you specialise in again?'

'Orthopaedics.' This was it, Hayden thought. He'd be bound to mention Annie now.

'Oh, that's right,' was all Adam said, but the tone of his voice had changed to one of avoidance.

Hayden wanted to know about his relationship with Annie yet at the same time he didn't. Just the thought of Annie with Adam was enough to turn his stomach.

There was an uncomfortable pause while Hayden mentally searched for a topic. 'Did you hear Rowena's getting married?'

'Yeah, my mum forwarded the wedding invitation. Stupid move on Ro's part.'

'Well, she doesn't seem to think so.'

'I haven't seen Ro in years. How old is she now?'

'Twenty-seven.'

'Wow. Last I saw of her, she had braces and acne.'

Hayden laughed. 'Seems like yesterday and now she's getting married.' He shook his head and rubbed his fingers through his hair. Leaning back in his chair, he hoped his next question came out with the required amount of nonchalance. 'Are you coming to the wedding?'

'Can't make it. I'm going to send her a reply tomorrow to let her know.'

'That's too bad. It would have been good to catch up in person.'

'Yeah. Listen, Hayd. I have to go. Duty calls.'

'Sure. Good to talk to you.' Hayden rang off, feeling more frustrated than he had before the call. He rested his elbows on the desk and buried his face in his hands. He felt…plagued by thoughts of Annie. During the day, when he went to sleep and now, after kissing her so completely, so passionately, it was getting worse.

He massaged his temples, trying to figure out what on earth he should do. He'd asked her to Rowena's wedding. He had to spend the weekend with her and *not* kiss her. He could do that. He was strong.

The wedding was two weeks away and until then he was determined to keep as far away from Annie as possible. She'd been right. It was the only way to ensure self-preservation.

Annie almost crawled up the walls on Friday and Saturday because of her imposed leave from the hospital. She read a book, watched television, went for runs, but nothing took her mind off Hayden for long.

By Saturday afternoon she'd had enough and caught a taxi to Natasha's house. Spending time with the Worthington kids helped to distract her—at least for a short time. She stayed for dinner and once the children were in bed, she sat down to talk with Brenton and Natasha.

'So…can we ask you about Hayden?' Brenton queried with a knowing grin after they'd had coffee.

Annie pointedly looked at her watch. 'Gee, is that the time? I'd better be getting home.'

Her friends laughed. 'Leave her alone, Brenton,' Natasha chided. 'Annie knows we're here to listen or discuss things but only when she's ready.'

'Thank you.'

Natasha leaned forward in her chair, her smile anxious. 'Ready?'

Annie laughed. 'Not yet.'

'That means something's happened.' Brenton rubbed his hands together delightedly. 'I'd just like to say right here and now that I think he's perfect for you.'

'You hardly know him,' she countered, not that bothered by the good-natured teasing.

'Our paths have crossed several times since he started working at the hospital on Monday. All I'm saying is that so far I like what I see.'

'And what's that?'

'He appears to be a man of integrity, high calibre and good taste. After all, my dear friend, if he's interested in you, he's showing good taste.'

Tears welled in Annie's eyes. 'Thank you.' She sighed and slumped back into the chair. 'I just don't want to get hurt again…and neither does he.'

'You said he'd been married before,' Natasha commented.

'I also said I didn't want to discuss it,' Annie reminded them with a smile. She had questions of her own. Questions about his marriage, but more questions about his daughter. How had she died? Had there been an accident? Four weeks old. Even to think about it broke her heart. It was no wonder Hayden had blocked himself off from ever going there again. She forced herself to focus on what her friends were saying.

'OK. We'll change the subject. Did Lily tell you she's got a real gig playing her guitar in an amateur musical group?'

Annie's sigh was heartfelt. 'Yes, she did mention it. I'm so proud of her.' The conversation continued on neutral topics until it was really time for her to leave. On the way home, she stopped by the shops and picked up the ingredients for a hot toddy.

It was almost eleven o'clock when Annie put the shopping bags down to unlock her apartment door. When the stairwell door opened, she knew instinctively it was Hayden. The hairs on the back of her neck prickled with apprehension, wondering how this meeting would go. She turned to face him.

'Hi.'

'Hi.'

'Just getting home from the hospital?' He looked awful, she thought.

'Yes. You've been out?'

'Dinner with the Worthingtons.'

He nodded. 'Hope you had a good time.' He paused by his apartment door and looked at her. 'Feeling better?'

'Yes.'

'Really? You look washed out.'

She smiled tiredly. 'You're so full of compliments.' She paused, not wanting him to be unduly worried about her. 'I'm over the stomach virus, if that's your concern.'

'But you haven't been sleeping,' he added.

'No.' She looked away, not wanting him to realise *he* was the reason why she hadn't been sleeping.

'Me neither.' The words were said so softly that for a moment she thought she'd imagined it. She glanced up at his face and saw the anguish there. She knew that anguish because it matched her own.

She unlocked her door. 'We have to get past this, Hayden.'

'You're right.'

'I'm going to make a hot toddy and actually get some sleep tonight.'

'Good for you.' He smiled.

Annie hesitated for a moment. 'Would you like to join me?' At the look of desire that briefly flashed in his eyes she quickly added, 'You look as though *you* could use a good night's sleep as well. Just a drink, Hayden, but I understand if you'd rather not.'

'That's just the problem, Annie.' He took a step towards her. 'I'd like nothing more than to join you.'

'Surely we can control ourselves? We're both adults and we have to get past this,' she said again.

Hayden took a deep breath and slowly exhaled. 'OK. A drink and we'll stick to neutral topics.'

'Good idea.' She opened the door and picked up her

shopping bags. Hayden left his briefcase just inside her door and followed her through to the kitchen. They worked together in harmony and soon were sitting down, Annie on the sofa, Hayden in the chair, with the coffee-table between them, sipping the warm drink.

'This is nice,' he said after a few mouthfuls.

'Tastes great.'

'I meant you and I.'

'Oh.' Annie bit her lip at the misunderstanding, immediately thinking that her reply could also apply to them. Hayden *did* taste great. 'Yes. Yes it is.'

'We can do this, Annie.' He took another sip and relaxed back in the chair. 'We can be friends.'

'Of course we can,' she agreed. Even as she said the words, she hoped rather than knew they were true. As they'd agreed, they talked on neutral topics and were surprised to find many common opinions.

As he was leaving some time later, at the door he picked up his briefcase and looked down at her. 'Thanks. This was good.'

'It was.'

Silence hung in the air and awkwardness started to stretch between them. If he took one step forward, it would be nothing for her to stand on tiptoe and press her mouth to his. Instead, Hayden forced his smile to stay in place and took one step backwards.

'Hope you sleep well, Annie.' His tone was soft and endearing.

'You, too.' She ignored the tingles, the flood of longing and need that ripped through her. As soon as he stepped out of her doorway, she shut the door. The muted noises that came through the walls settled her a little and only when all was quiet next door did she close her eyes to try and sleep.

As Hayden lay in bed, he laced his hands behind his head and closed his eyes. A smile tugged at his lips and he realised he was insanely pleased that she'd got rid of Adam's photograph from her love-heart frame. The Worthington family in that frame he could definitely cope with. Taking in a deep breath, he felt himself relax.

CHAPTER SIX

FOR the next week, Annie only saw Hayden when necessary. Although they smiled at each other, treated each other like they did every other member of staff, they were both lying to themselves.

On Monday, they reviewed Mr Andersen together in the clinic, with Annie escorting their elderly patient out so she wouldn't have to stay and make idle chit-chat with Hayden.

'How can we possibly be...be...*friends* when I feel *so* much more?' she asked her reflection two days before she was supposed to accompany him to his sister's wedding. He hadn't sought her out, hadn't said anything more about the wedding or whether or not he still wanted her to go with him.

The only way she'd slept had been to run herself ragged during the day. Expending all her energy had become a form of self-preservation in itself.

Tomorrow was going to be the worst. Unfilled Friday, she'd decided to call it. For some reason Hayden had rostered her off and she had the entire day to herself. Well, if exhaustion was going to be the only way for her to get through the day, she would fill it to the hilt with activities guaranteed to make even the most insomniac sufferer sleep.

Jogging in the morning, a workout at the gym, doing an entire grocery shop in less than twenty minutes, a few games of pool to try and relax her. She *had* to fill every second of the day, and when she got home from work on Thursday evening she sat down to write up a detailed schedule of events.

The knock at the door just after half past nine startled her. She was just rearranging the time frame of six thirty-seven to six fifty-two, trying to decide the best way to completely fill this time gap.

'Hayden!' She gasped after opening the door. 'Is something wrong?'

'No. I just realised I hadn't told you what time we'd be leaving tomorrow.'

'Sorry?'

'We'll need to get away fairly early. After all, we don't want to get stuck in peak-hour traffic.'

'What?' If she'd been confused before, it was nothing compared to now.

'It's either that or leave after ten o'clock, but then we risk Sydney's peak-hour traffic in the evening.'

'*What* on earth are you talking about?'

'My sister's wedding.'

'Is on Saturday. Tomorrow is Friday.'

'That's right.' He was looking at her as though she had two heads. 'The wedding is on Saturday.'

'So why do we have to leave tomorrow and what does Sydney traffic—?' She stopped as his words caught up with her. 'Your sister lives in *Sydney*?' she asked incredulously.

'Yes.' Now it was his turn to frown. 'Didn't I mention that?'

'No.'

He smiled apologetically. 'Sorry. I rostered both of us off for the weekend as we'll need to drive to Sydney tomorrow and drive back on Sunday.'

'Why drive? Why not fly?'

'I prefer to drive,' he said nonchalantly.

'So we're driving to Sydney tomorrow,' she stated.

'Yes. You didn't have anything scheduled for tomorrow?'

She thought of the excessive list she'd been poring over for the past few hours. 'No.' She got to spend the day in a car with Hayden! She smiled and then a giggle escaped. She got to spend an entire day with Hayden—all to herself. The giggle turned to a laugh as the pressure she'd been feeling for the past few weeks came bubbling up to the surface.

'Annie?'

She leaned against the door, laughing with relief.

'Are you OK?'

'Yes.' She wiped the tears from her eyes. 'Yes, I'm fine. Whew! I needed that.'

'I'm glad...' Hayden's smile was cute but confused. 'I think.'

'So, what time do you want to leave?'

'I thought if we could get away by about four or four-thirty in the morning, we should get into Sydney around ten hours later.'

Annie thought for a moment. 'Sure. Four o'clock should be fine.'

'Good. I'll knock on your door at four.'

She giggled at the rhyme. 'See you then.' As she was about to shut the door, Hayden looked as though he was going to say something. She stopped but he only smiled so she continued to close the door.

'Yes!' She punched the air with her fist and almost danced over to her ridiculous schedule. 'Your services are no longer required.' She took the piece of paper and ripped it up with great delight. Next, she danced over to the phone and called Natasha to tell her the news.

'Well, well, well,' Natasha said. 'Two whole days stuck in a car with the man of your dreams.'

'I know.' Annie cradled the phone between her shoulder and ear, packing as she spoke to her friend.

'Annie?' Natasha's voice was cautious.

'Hmm?'

'I just said ''the man of your dreams'', and you agreed.'

'So?' Her stomach twisted with pleasure and uncontrollable excitement as well as trepidation and horror.

'*So?* Is Hayden the man of your dreams?'

'I don't know, Tash,' she wailed, and slumped down onto the futon. 'I'm not sure how I feel. One minute he's completely irresistible and the next he's aloof. He'll smile at me in a friendly way and the next instant we're staring at each other as though we want nothing more than to tear each other's clothes off.'

'Sounds promising,' Natasha murmured.

'Tell me what to do. You have to tell me what to do!'

'Don't think about it. You've got him all to yourself for a few days. Away from the hospital, away from the rest of Geelong. So just try to relax and enjoy yourself.'

'That's the thing, though. The more I enjoy myself around him, the more I relax, the more I gaze into his hypnotic blue eyes…the more I feel myself falling in love with him.'

'So?'

'So he doesn't want to get married *or* have children.' Annie closed her eyes, desperately wanting to know more about Hayden's daughter.

'Really?' Natasha was astounded.

'Don't say anything, Tash. Oh, I'm so confused. I can't wait to leave but…'

'Does he know it's your birthday on Saturday?'

'No, but it doesn't matter. I don't want to overshadow his sister's wedding.'

'You'd hardly do that. You're not that type of person.'

'I think you're right. I think I should just let go and try to enjoy myself.'

Her friend chuckled. 'You do that. What are you going to wear to the wedding?'

Annie sat bolt upright. 'Oh, no.'

'Oh, Annie, you haven't.'

'Yes, I have.' She placed her free hand over her face. 'I've been so wrapped up with work and trying not to think about Hayden or anything to do with him that I didn't go and buy a dress! I can't believe it. I don't have anything to wear to the wedding. What am I going to do?' she wailed. 'We'll be leaving in about six hours' time!'

'I'd bring some of my dresses over but Brenton's at the hospital and Aunt Jude is out on a date.'

'Jude's on a date?'

'Yeah. Pretty cool, but I'll tell you about it later. I can't leave the children.'

'I wouldn't want you to. It's just gone ten o'clock so it's too late for you to come out anyway. I'll just have to go shopping on Saturday morning.'

'What time is the wedding?'

Annie grimaced. 'I hope it's not a breakfast wedding.'

'Me, too. Oh, Annie. Maybe you'll get some time once you get into Sydney tomorrow night. The shops should be open, and by leaving at four in the morning…'

'You're right. I'll just buy something there. Other than that, I'll be wearing a black skirt and a bra as I don't have any nice tops.'

'Hayden *definitely* won't be able to resist you if you wear that.'

Both women laughed. 'Don't want to outshine the bride,' Annie added. 'Seriously, though, I'll be fine.'

'OK. I'll let you go and finish packing. Have a fantastic time and let us know when you arrive so we know you're there safely.'

'Will do.' Annie paused for a moment. 'Thanks, Tash. You and Brenton are the best friends a girl could ask for.'

'Hey—what's this *friends* garbage? Don't you remember my children officially adopted you last Christmas? We're *family*!'

Tears welled in Annie's eyes. 'You're right. We *are* family. How stupid of me to forget.'

'Well…don't let it happen again.'

'I won't.'

'Promise you'll call?'

'Promise.'

'All right. Drive safely and have a *wonderful* time.'

'I will. Love you.'

'You, too.'

Annie rang off and looked at the phone. Both Brenton and Natasha were only children as well, so they knew exactly how she felt not having any siblings. How could she have forgotten the ceremony they'd had after Christmas lunch as the Worthington children had declared her an official member of their family? She vowed never to do it again.

One day, hopefully in the not-too-distant future, she would find her perfect match and start her new life, a new family she could share with the Worthingtons.

Was Hayden that man?

Was *he* her perfect match?

She really hoped so because, whether she liked it or not, she was falling in love with him.

Annie woke up just after midnight and checked the clock yet again.

'I'm never going to get to sleep at this rate,' she mumbled as she turned over, punched her pillow and tried to settle back down. Although she'd set her alarm clock for three-thirty, giving her enough time to shower and pack those last-minute things, she was still waking up every twenty minutes thinking she'd slept through the alarm.

She sighed with frustration as she closed her eyes once more and drifted off.

Twenty minutes later on the dot she sat bolt upright, checked the clock and then settled back against the pillows as her crazy heart rate slowly returned to normal after the initial fright that she'd missed the alarm.

'I give up.' She flung back the cotton sheet before stalking into the kitchen. It was madness trying to sleep, even though her body told her she was exhausted. She drank a glass of water, leaned against the kitchen bench and closed her eyes, trying to figure out what she should do.

A loud ringing sound woke her and she jerked upright, surprised to find she'd been sleeping at the kitchen bench.

It was the alarm! No, it was the phone. She raced to the lounge room and silenced it.

'Dr Beresford,' she mumbled, forcing her sluggish brain to work as she listened carefully to what the nurse was saying. 'OK. Give me fifteen minutes.' She replaced the receiver and hurried to her bedroom to dress. A birthday party had apparently got out of control and the A and E department was now flooded with casualties.

She grabbed her keys and headed out. She hoped she'd be able to find a taxi at this time of night but the streets were well lit and it wasn't that far to walk. When she reached the footpath, there wasn't a taxi in sight so she started walking. She'd just reached the corner of her street when a car pulled to the kerb beside her.

She looked over her shoulder, slightly startled, and desperately tried to recall the self-defence moves she'd learned over five or so years ago.

'Annie!'

She inwardly relaxed at the sound of Hayden's voice, even though he sounded ready to explode.

'What on earth do you think you're doing?' He'd stopped the car, opened the driver's door and was yelling at her. 'Get inside this car right now.' He couldn't believe her stupidity at walking alone in the dark. A primal protective urge welled up inside, taking him completely by surprise. As she climbed in the car, he quickly told himself that he'd feel this way for any woman of his acquaintance doing the same stupid thing. She was nothing special.

The instant the thought came into his head, his heart refuted it. If she really *was* nothing special, why was he so determined to keep his distance? She wanted marriage, he reminded himself, and he didn't *do* marriage.

Her subtle perfume, which made her smell as sweet as a spring day, wound around him as she clicked her seat belt into place. It was enough to drive a man instantly insane with longing, and although he'd been schooling himself for the long drive to Sydney they were yet to undertake, he now wasn't so sure he'd survive.

She'd asked him to keep his hands and his lips to himself and he'd thought he had enough self-control to do so, yet when she smelt *this* good, especially at such an early hour of the morning, he knew he had an internal fight coming if he was going to stay true to his word.

Thankfully, right now it was only a short trip to the hospital.

'Some days I wonder if you've any sense at all,' he growled as he started the engine and pulled the dark green Jaguar away from the kerb.

'I was going to look for a taxi along the way,' she protested.

He muttered something else beneath his breath and she was almost sure she didn't want to know what it was.

'Nice car,' she said, glad the convertible roof was firmly in place. 'Rental?'

'No. Mine.'

'I haven't seen it in the tenant garages before.'

'It's been at the mechanic's for the past few weeks.' At her raised eyebrows he continued, 'The car was involved in an accident before I left Perth so I had it brought over by rail and delivered straight to a specialised repairer.'

'You had an accident? Well, that fills me with confidence.' Her tone was dry but teasing.

'I never said *I* had the accident. I said the *car* was involved in an accident. And besides, driving with me to the hospital is probably a lot safer than walking the streets in the early hours of the morning.'

Hayden parked the car and once Annie was out, he locked it and started off towards the emergency entrance. The sound of wailing sirens in the distance could be heard as the ambulances closed in on them.

'Looks as though we may not be leaving at four o'clock after all,' she mumbled as they walked in through the door.

'We'll just have to play things by ear.'

They went to the nurses' station where Brenton was gathering people around to brief them. 'All right, people. Listen up. Just after midnight an emergency call was logged from an eighteenth birthday party where over three hundred people had turned up.'

'So many?' Natasha asked.

'Apparently it had been advertised over the internet, which meant anyone could turn up,' Brenton answered. 'We've already have a few casualties in but the ambulance crews have reported there's plenty more to come. As you can hear, the sirens aren't too far away. Tash, you and the triage sister handle the incoming cases.' He checked his clipboard and continued down the list, giving people their jobs.

'Where's Paul Jamieson? Anyone seen him?'

'He's on his way,' Deb, one of the nurses, reported.

'Good. As usual, both elective and emergency theatres are available. Let's get going.' The ambulances pulled up at the door and for the next few hours Annie and Hayden saw one patient after another.

Even though A and E was hectic, she instinctively knew where Hayden was most of the time.

'Has anyone seen Professor Robinson?' Wesley asked, as another stretcher was wheeled into the treatment room.

'Just gone into emergency theatre one,' Annie replied, and before anyone could say anything else she pulled on a pair of gloves and turned her attention to the patient.

The first she knew Hayden was out of Theatre was forty-five minutes later when Hayden walked into examination cubicle nine.

'Got half an hour to spare?'

'Just let me finish up these notes. What's on offer?' She tried to ignore the tightening in her stomach as his deep, vibrant tone washed over her.

'Badly fractured femur. Heavy loss of blood.'

She signed her name and carried the notes out to the

nurses' station to return them. 'Sounds like fun,' she replied lethargically. 'Let's go.'

Soon they were scrubbed and in Theatre, all previous fatigue disappearing as they both concentrated. She assisted Hayden in her usual efficient manner as he quickly found the offending artery and clamped it. 'Right. Now, let's get down to business.' Together they debrided the wound before fixing the fractured bone back together with a Grosse and Kempf nailing rod.

The phone rang and the scout nurse answered it. 'It's Paul Jamieson,' she told them. 'He needs one of you urgently.'

Hayden's gaze met Annie's. 'Who's he again?'

'Paul Jamieson. General surgeon,' she explained.

'You go, Annie. I'll be fine now.' Their gazes met for a brief second and she couldn't resist teasing him a bit.

'Thanks for inviting me along.' Immediately his blue depths twinkled and she knew he was smiling beneath his mask.

'I know how to show a girl a good time.' He glanced around at the other women in the theatre. 'Don't I, ladies?'

There were several murmurs of 'yes' and the tension everyone had been feeling for the past few hours started to lift.

'Don't have too much fun while I'm gone,' Annie warned as she degowned and walked out of Theatres. She headed upstairs to the elective theatres where Paul was waiting for her.

'This man's arm is busted up so badly I needed someone to have a look immediately.'

'Wesley?'

'He's stuck in Theatre with another emergency.'

Annie scrubbed and gowned, heading into the operating room with Paul.

'Meet Mr Jock McInlay, who apparently is affectionately known to his friends as Hammer.' Paul indicated the anaesthetised man on the operating table.

'Hammer? I don't think I want to know how he got *that* nickname,' Annie replied.

'He's a twenty-five-year-old party goer who loves basketball and drinking games as well as lying beneath the tyres of four-wheel-drives while someone else drives over him—at least, that's what we assume because that's where he was found.'

'What's the damage?' Annie peered at the arm and shook her head. 'X-rays?'

'Here, Doctor.' One of the theatre nurses put up X-rays and Annie peered at them.

'Three lacerations to the abdomen—all quite severe—and before you ask...' he held up a hand to stop any questions '...we're not exactly sure what happened. Fractured metatarsals, fractured tibia and I'd say that shoulder is definitely dislocated.'

'You've got that right. I'm going to need Hayden in here. Ask him to come the instant he's finished.'

'Yes, Doctor,' the nurse replied.

'So he's stable?'

'As stable as I can make him. No offending arteries if that's what you mean.'

Annie nodded and received a report from the anaesthetist. 'All right. Let's get to work.'

The arm was indeed in a bad way but after consulting the X-rays again she saw that the neck of humerus wasn't fractured and so relocated the shoulder back into place.

'Ooh, I hate those crunching noises you orthopods make. You know, Annie, for someone your size, I'm surprised you've got the oomph to do a lot of the heavy work involved in your speciality.'

'Ingenuity, Paul. That's all it takes.'

'You should have chosen general surgery instead of orthopaedics.' He wiggled his eyebrows up and down. 'Then I could have...guided you.'

Annie laughed. 'To where? Your bed?'

Paul laughed back and so did several of the staff. 'Ah, Annie. You know me too well.'

'We all do, Paul. Your reputation as the hospital's worst flirt was determined years ago.'

'Still having fun, Annie?' Hayden asked from the doorway as he walked across to Annie's side. Once more their gazes met above their masks and this time she saw a warning in his eyes. She frowned a little, wondering why.

'Yes, and you're just in time to join in.'

Hayden turned his gaze from hers to the man on the other side of the table. 'You must be Paul Jamieson.'

'That's right.' Paul nodded and then briefed Hayden on Hammer, the nurse making sure the relevant X-rays were up on the viewer for Hayden to peruse.

'What have you got?'

Together they looked at the arm and managed to unmangle it. 'We'll need someone from Vascular to check this out,' he commented.

'Patient is stable from an orthopaedic point of view,' Annie said. 'Patient is all yours, Paul.'

'Thank you, Annie, dearest, and you, Hayden. Sorry we're not meeting under better circumstances.'

Hayden didn't say anything but instead walked out of Theatre. 'Next patient?'

'Yes.'

They degowned and headed back to A and E. She was just about to ask him what was wrong when he said softly, 'What's going on between you and the blond giant?'

'Pardon?' She looked at him in surprise.

'You heard me.'

'Nothing. Why should I care about Paul Jamieson?'

'You seemed quite…chummy with him.'

Annie laughed. 'That's just Paul. He flirts with anything in a skirt.'

'You're wearing trousers,' he pointed out.

Annie stopped in the stairwell and looked at Hayden. 'You sound…jealous,' she ventured slowly.

'No. Not jealous,' he remarked as he continued down the stairs. 'Just protective of my staff.'

Annie hid a knowing smile. 'I'll remember to let Wesley know.'

Hayden rounded on her as she came down the last step. 'You know what I mean, Annie.' He took a step forward, obviously trying to intimidate her, but she was too tired for games and stood her ground. They were almost nose to nose and slowly the smile she'd been trying to hide started to slip onto her lips.

'You certainly *sound* jealous. It's OK, Hayden. I won't let it go to my head.'

'You're impossible in this mood.' He turned and opened the door before walking out into the corridor.

Annie chuckled. 'Oh, how you make my head spin with all these compliments.'

'You're fatigued, Annie. Perhaps you should take a break.'

'I'm not fatigued. I'm releasing tension. There's a difference.'

'Teasing me is releasing tension?'

'Hey, it's working for me.' He glared at her and she smiled back. 'Now, I believe I had a patient waiting to see me a few hours ago. I'd better chase him up.'

An hour later the patients were still coming in.

'What on earth happened at this party?' Annie asked Natasha as they sat down for two minutes to quickly drink a much-needed cup of coffee.

'A brawl, basically.'

The triage sister walked into the room. 'You're on, ladies.'

'Thanks.' Natasha stood. 'So much for your quiet day driving.'

Annie glanced at the clock. It was just after eight o'clock and she felt as though she'd been in Theatre for ever.

'You said it, my friend.' Annie stood. 'Let's get back to the trenches.'

Soon she was back in Theatre, debriding another frac-tured leg before reducing the bone back into position with plates and screws. An hour later she started to close when a call came through to say Hayden needed her in theatre two with him.

She finished suturing and then stapled the wound closed before walking from the theatre, ripping off her theatre garb as she went and dumping it into the specially marked bin. She was scrubbed and with him fifteen minutes after the call.

'About time. I thought you'd never get here. It appears Mr Bouchard has indeed shattered his pelvis as well as most of his ribs, his scapula and his tibia.'

'Are you going to leave the pelvis for a few days? See if it settles?'

'Yes. He'll be fine in traction until we return on Monday.'

Annie nodded and they started the operation. They ap-plied an external fixator to the patient's tibia and pinned his scapula.

'Yes. I'd like to see him on Monday morning during ward round,' Hayden remarked as they strapped Mr Bouchard's ribs. 'And I wouldn't be at all surprised if we're in Theatre not long after that.'

'I'll take care of the paperwork,' Annie replied. After Theatre, she returned to the female changing rooms, dredg-ing up the energy from somewhere to shower and dress, very thankful that the early morning call was now over. She was attempting to comb her unruly curls into some sort of order when Deb came in.

'I hear you and Hayden are off somewhere together this weekend.'

It was then Annie recalled Hayden saying he would look at the pelvic fracture once they'd returned on Monday. She wondered if she could try and save herself by stating that although both of them were rostered off for the weekend, that didn't mean they would be spending it together.

'Don't bother to deny it, Annie,' Deb held up a hand. 'You look like a rabbit caught in a trap. I just thought you should know the gossip is spreading around.'

'Like wildfire.' Annie rolled her eyes and closed her locker.

'Does going away for the weekend mean it's serious between you two?'

Annie shrugged and looked at the nurse.

'Come on, Annie. We've worked together for about ten years. I listen to the gossip, true, but most of the time I don't put any faith in it. If I have a question, I'll come right out and ask you—or the person involved.'

'True,' Annie replied. 'It's nothing special. We're going to Sydney for his sister's wedding.'

'Woo-hoo. Meeting the family. You're *that* serious.'

'It isn't like that.' Although she wished it was.

'Yeah? Well, why did he look as though he was ready to strangle Paul earlier?'

'Were you in Theatre with Paul? I don't remember seeing—'

'No, but I heard about it.'

'He wasn't ready to strangle Paul. In fact, Paul was…you know.' She shrugged. 'Just being Paul.'

'Harmless flirting,' Deb stated, and looked down at her hands.

'Yes.'

'I don't think our new professor liked it at all.' There was a hint of something in Deb's voice. It was strained and Annie suddenly looked at her, as though for the first time.

'Obviously, he wasn't the only one. Deb, are you and Paul involved?'

It was Deb's turn to look pale. 'Yes.'

'Wow. How has *this* been kept a secret?'

'With extreme difficulty,' Deb replied. 'And we'd like to keep it that way.'

'So it's serious?'

'Yes.'

Annie smiled. 'Good for you, Deb—and Paul. I thought he'd *never* settle down.'

'We're getting old, Annie.'

They both laughed. 'Tell me about it.'

'Oh, that's right. Tomorrow's your birthday. Have a great time.'

Annie headed for the door. 'I will, and thanks for the tip-off about the gossip.' She walked out with a mild spring in her step. It was nearly ten o'clock in the morning and they still had a ten or so hour drive to Sydney to complete. She should be feeling exhausted!

She organised the paperwork for the possibility of Mr Bouchard going to Theatre on Monday before heading to the A and E nurses' station to check that everything was all right. As she neared she saw Natasha deep in discussion with Hayden, and when her friend saw her she mumbled something and then Hayden turned to look at her.

'Now, I know the rest of the hospital is gossiping about me but I thought you two were above that,' she teased.

Natasha laughed and gave her a hug. 'Drive safely,' she said. 'And don't forget to call when you get there.'

'I will, Mum,' Annie promised. She looked at Hayden. 'Are we free to go?'

'Yes. Triage Sister and Brenton have announced the situation is under control. We'll leave the ward round to Wesley and sneak off while we can.' Hayden was making no effort to hide the fact that he and Annie were leaving together and she felt a strange sense of…empowerment wash over her. He obviously wasn't concerned at the two of them being gossiped about and she decided that for the moment she wouldn't care either.

They walked out of the hospital together. 'We'll pick up our bags, then get under way.'

'Sounds good.'

'Excellent.'

They reached the inner roads of Melbourne just past eleven o'clock, with rush-hour traffic well and truly over.

'Well, at least we got that bit right,' Annie murmured as she settled back against the comfortable headrest. 'What a morning.'

'Not exactly what I'd had in mind.' Hayden laughed. 'Sleep if you can because we will be changing places later.' He switched on some music and with the soothing strains of Vivaldi swirling around her, Annie closed her eyes.

She managed to doze, feeling a little self-conscious at first but then exhaustion hit and she slept soundly.

'Hey, sleepyhead.' Three hours later Hayden stopped the car, unbuckled his seat belt and turned to look at the woman beside him. Annie looked gorgeous as she slept, her pillow up against the window, her face cushioned at an odd angle. Her curls were tangled, her body was relaxed and he felt an imperceptible tightening in his gut. She looked young and vulnerable and he couldn't believe she was almost forty.

'Annie?' Even the sound of her name on his lips felt right. He reached out a hand and gently touched her shoulder. She slept on. Leaning a little closer, not wanting to give her a fright, he worked hard to resist the urge to kiss her awake, even though her delectable mouth was begging for his touch.

'Wake up, sleepyhead.'

Still nothing. Her lips parted as she sighed dreamily, and the control he'd been exhibiting snapped.

With his heart tattooing a wild and stimulating rhythm, Hayden leaned even closer and pressed his warm mouth to hers, savouring the forbidden contact.

She stretched langorously and opened her mouth beneath this. She moaned and shifted, deepening the kiss, opening herself up to him completely, abandoning every scrap of self-preservation she'd gathered around her.

Never, in his life, had he been kissed with such... honesty.

His good intentions, his plans, his ideals disappeared in

the sensual haze that was Annie Beresford. He felt himself going down for the count.

Once, twice, three times, and then Hayden felt it.

The fine hairline crack through the thick ice that surrounded his heart.

CHAPTER SEVEN

HAYDEN hadn't even realised Annie had made it over the wall that protected the ice...but she had. Somehow she had. He felt invaded but as his mouth moved over hers once more, the warmth of her pressed against him, he knew it was an invasion he'd unconsciously authorised.

'Mmm.' Annie shifted in her seat, breaking the kiss to allow a yawn to escape her luscious pink lips. 'Nice dream,' she murmured before turning a little and opening her eyes a fraction. 'Hey, there.' She smiled at him and he felt his heart fill with pleasure—pleasure he knew he had to somehow control.

She stretched her arms up to the soft top before flexing her cramped neck. The way Hayden was looking at her took her completely by surprise. It was the look that said he wanted to kiss her for the rest of her life, but she knew she was mistaken because Hayden didn't believe in happy ever after. She clamped down on the hope that had sprung up— probably due to the dream she'd had where he'd been kissing her with a depth she'd never felt before.

Self-preservation, she reminded herself quickly.

'Wha—?' Her voice stuck and she cleared her throat. Where are we?'

'Wangaratta.'

'Wow. What's the time?'

'Almost two o'clock.'

'You made good time.' She moved in her seat and Hayden thankfully leaned back. The scent of him had been driving her senses crazy, along with the closeness of his body. All of this, in the confines of the car, were perfect inducements to a nice romantic moment—one they were *not* going to share.

Was Annie aware that he'd just kissed her awake? He wasn't sure. Hayden cleared his throat. 'Hungry?'

She thought for a moment and then nodded. 'Yes.'

'Good. Natasha told me this was a good place to eat.' He pointed to the café they'd stopped beside.

'Yes. As a matter of fact it is.' She climbed from the car, glad of the opportunity to stretch properly while she waited for him to walk around the car to her side.

'You've been here before?'

'Yes. Natasha used to live here, and a lot of her friends still do. Kelly and Matt Bentley are doctors in Bright, which is about forty-five minutes that way.' She pointed in the relevant direction.

Hayden smiled at her as they went inside the café. 'I know where Bright is, Annie.'

'Good. Perhaps on the way back, if we make good time, we can arrange to stop in and see them.'

He thought for a moment. She wanted him to meet her friends? Was that a good sign or one that meant she was getting too close? He shrugged. 'We'll see.'

Annie noted his reluctance. It had only been a suggestion and one which she'd made off the top of her head. 'I usually try and drop in when I'm around this area.' She tried to keep her tone nonchalant as they were shown to a table. 'We don't have to.'

She was making him feel guilty now, and it was the last thing he wanted. He picked up the menu and studied it intently.

While they ate, the atmosphere was a little strained to begin with but slowly they found the camaraderie they usually enjoyed. When they were finished they went outside and Hayden tossed Annie his car keys.

'My turn?' She couldn't contain her excitement.

'It's what you've been waiting for, isn't it?'

'You betcha.' She climbed into the driver's seat. 'Fasten

your seat belt, mate. I'm gonna show you what this car can do.'

'You also get to pay for any tickets.'

'Deal.'

Before she started the engine, Annie turned to him and asked, 'Do you trust me with your car?'

Hayden smiled, realising that he did. It surprised him. 'I wouldn't let you drive it otherwise.'

'I see. I thought you were letting me drive so you could take a break.'

'That, too.' He watched as she rubbed her hands around the steering-wheel almost caressing it. 'What are you doing?'

'Taking my time. Getting to know him.'

'Her.'

'Pardon?'

'The car, it's a *her*. All cars are female.'

'Says who?' Annie took a breath and started the engine. The purr was faultless and, after adjusting and checking the mirrors, she pulled carefully out into the traffic.

'Says everyone.'

'Says every male, you mean.'

'It's just a fact, Annie. That's why guys can spend so much time with their cars. They never nag, they never complain, they're always there when a guy needs them.'

Annie threw back her head and laughed. 'Sounds boring,' she retorted. 'Besides, I wasn't talking about the car.'

'When?'

'When I said I was getting to know him.' She glanced across and laughed. 'Don't look so horrified.' She laughed again and pointed to the pillow. 'Why don't you get some sleep? You'll need to keep your mental strength up if you're going to successfully avoid all the probing questions I have for you.'

'I think I'd better stay awake and keep an eye on you. Who knows what crazy things you'll do while I'm asleep?'

'Aw, come on Hayden. I thought you trusted me.'

'With the *car*, Annie. With the *car*.'

She laughed and so did he. They talked for a while and she was glad of the company, but after half an hour or so Hayden rested his head back against the headrest and closed his eyes.

'Sing to me, Annie.'

'What?' His request startled her a little.

'Sing to me. You have a lovely voice.'

'How do you know?'

He smiled but didn't open his eyes. 'The wall between our apartments is rather thin.'

'Oh. I'm sorry if I disturbed you.'

'Not at all. I've enjoyed each and every tune I've heard.'

'Quite an eclectic mix, I'm afraid.'

'Nothing wrong with that.'

'OK. What would you like? Country? Rock 'n' roll? Ballad?'

'Ballad, please.'

Annie thought for a moment, going through a selection of tunes in her head before settling on one of her favourites. She sang clearly and with passion, enjoying herself long after Hayden had dropped off to sleep.

She allowed herself to daydream…to pretend that she and Hayden, as a couple, were driving to Sydney to see the family. Their children would be in the back, lulled asleep by their mother's singing, just as their father had been.

She sighed and shook herself, dismissing the notion. A tear welled up and slid down her cheek. It wouldn't do for her vision to blur while she was driving so she forced herself to think about something else. Something uninteresting and benign—like Mr Bouchard's impending pelvic surgery.

An hour later Hayden stirred and they continued to swap every few hours to ensure they stayed refreshed. As night began to fall, weariness began to set in. Hayden was driving the last leg as he knew the way to his parents' house.

'Talk to me, Annie. Keep me alert.'

'OK.' She thought for a moment before asking quietly, 'Who was driving your car when it was in the accident?'

'Interesting topic of conversation.'

'I did warn you I had some probing questions. Are you going to answer them?'

It was a test and he knew it. 'My ex-wife,' he replied eventually.

'She had this car?'

'For a while.'

'I was under the impression the two of you had been divorced for quite some time now.'

'Almost eight years.'

'And you still have contact?'

'Let's just say she…borrowed it, without my permission, while I was overseas at a conference before Christmas.'

'She *stole* it?'

'Yes but not technically. She still had a key and…I didn't press charges.'

'So she stole your car and then smashed it?'

'Yes.'

'Was she hurt?'

'No.'

'Were you?' Annie shifted in her chair to look at him.

He was silent for a moment and she wondered if she'd pushed too far, too fast.

'I wasn't in the car.'

'Don't be obtuse, Hayden.'

'Her…vindictiveness hurt, yes.'

'Will you tell me about her?'

'Why the sudden interest?'

'It's not sudden, Hayden. These questions and a lot more have been buzzing around in my mind for a while.' When he didn't say anything, she took a deep breath and plunged right in. 'There's something…*amazing* happening between us, Hayden, and denying it or saying that we're going to be just good friends is ridiculous.'

'I suppose you want to know about my daughter as well.'
His tone was indignant.

'Yes.'

'Why? Why can't we leave it in the past?'

'There are some things that can't be left there if you're
going to get on with your life.'

'I'm alive, aren't I? I've continued to live.'

'Are you really living, or merely existing?' she asked.
She knew she had him riled now and was sorry because
she hadn't meant to. 'I'm not criticising,' she added hastily.

'No?'

'No. Our pasts make us who we are today. It's what we
do with that knowledge, that emotion, that experience,
which counts.' The knuckles of his hands were almost
white as they gripped the wheel. 'I know you feel as though
I'm criticising you, but I'm not. Honestly.' She shifted uncomfortably in her seat and sighed. 'I'm actually criticising
myself.'

'Meaning?'

'Meaning we all have our problems. I haven't had the
best life but it's something I try to figure out, without
dwelling on it, and make the best of. I've been unlucky in
love more times than I care to admit but, still, I keep coming back for more. I need my head read.' She mumbled the
last but he heard.

'So why do you?'

'Keep coming back? It's not a choice. I met you, didn't
I? I didn't ask for this attraction to be there between us,
but it is, Hayden. The point is, I'm trying to make the most
out of my life.'

'And if you don't end up getting married?'

'Then I don't end up getting married.'

'Wouldn't that break your heart?'

'Yes, but I know the people around who love me would
help me through. Look, sorry to sound all philosophical and
all that, but as far as I'm concerned, we're all just a dash.'

'Just a what?'

'Just a dash. You know, on tombstones there's the date you were born, then a dash and then the date you died. Life *is* that dash, Hayden, and I want to make sure it means something.'

Hayden turned right off the main road and into a suburban street. He turned left, then right and Annie felt herself calming down. He slowed and indicated, bringing the car to a stop in a tree-lined driveway outside a double-storey colonial home.

He cut the engine, undid his seat belt and turned to face her. Annie held her breath, desperately trying to gauge his mood, but it was dark and she could hardly see his face.

'I've heard what you've said and…maybe I do need to open up. It's just not something I'm good at.' He reached over and stroked a finger down her cheek. 'You're right, Annie. There is something…unique between us.' He cupped her face and urged her closer.

Her breathing increased and she leaned towards him, the seat belt stopping her. She quickly undid it and tilted her head back to accept his lips. The anticipation of their warmth, the trembling she would feel, the way his fingers would tighten imperceptibly in her hair… Everything. She wanted it all and she wanted it now.

She closed her eyes, her impatience growing with each passing second, and just as his mouth brushed lightly across hers he jerked back, severing the contact immediately. She opened her eyes and gazed out into the darkness of the car. 'Hayden?' she whispered, and then heard his door shut. He'd left?

Then she heard voices outside and realised his mother had come out to greet them. Annie closed her eyes and took a deep breath before climbing out of the car, a smile pasted in place.

'Welcome, dear. I'm Eloise, Hayden's mother.'

'Mum, this is Annie Beresford, a colleague of mine.'

Eloise took one of Annie's hands in hers and

squeezed it affectionately. 'We're delighted to have you. Come along inside and meet the rest of the family.'

The Robinson family had stayed up specifically to welcome them, and after a cool drink Annie pleaded fatigue and Eloise showed her to her room. After calling Natasha to let her know they'd arrived safely, Annie tried to settle down.

She'd been instantly envious of the close family atmosphere, never having experienced it herself. Her father was a workaholic and her stepmother was definitely not interested in anything other than what Annie's father's money could buy.

Here, although she admired the way the Robinsons had stayed up to greet one of their own, it made her feel like an outsider. Not wanting to intrude, she lay awake for at least the next hour, listening to the muted sounds of the family below.

What if she didn't end up marrying and having a family of her own? It was a valid question and one she'd tried hard not to consider. She guessed she would survive…somehow. She drifted into a restless sleep, positive she could actually hear her biological clock ticking.

Annie opened her eyes to the brilliance of morning sunshine peeking through the lacy curtains around the window. She frowned, wondering when she'd hung lacy curtains. They certainly weren't her style.

Slowly she eased herself up and glanced around the room, realising it wasn't her apartment. She was sleeping in one of Hayden's sisters' bedrooms at his parents' house. Annie flopped back onto the pillow for a moment, closing her eyes.

Knowing she couldn't sleep any longer, Annie climbed out of the fussy pink single bed and walked over to her bag. She'd been shown last night where the bathroom was, and as the clock beside the bed said it was just before six, Annie thought she'd take the opportunity to use the bathroom before other people woke. She had no idea how many guests were in the house but guaranteed, with the wedding today, the bathroom would soon be in high demand.

As she took out a fresh set of lacy underwear she remembered it was her birthday. Not just any birthday, but her *fortieth*. 'Happy birthday,' she whispered, and then laughed at how forlorn she sounded.

She *had* hoped that spending the day with Hayden would be a good present to herself, but after their discussion in the car and how she'd pressured him she wasn't sure what type of greeting she'd get from him this morning.

'One way to find out,' she mumbled, as she pulled out a short skirt and singlet top. The humidity in Sydney had been stifling last night, worse than she'd thought. She wanted to get out, go for a walk to clear her head before the rest of the day progressed.

She crept across the hall to the bathroom, locking the door after her, and proceeded to shower. Afterwards she towelled herself dry and had just finished putting on her underwear when a door opened and Hayden walked in, wearing only a pair of boxer shorts, rubbing his eyes.

'Hayden!'

His eyes snapped open, his hand dropped back to his side as he stared at Annie. She was vainly trying to clutch her clothes in front of her but as neither garment was long, they didn't hide much. He could still see her russet red lacy underwear quite clearly, as well as the rest of her gorgeous figure.

'Hayden!' she said again, momentarily glancing behind her at the door she'd come through from the hall.

'Uh…there are two doors.' He motioned to the one he'd just come through. 'One off the hallway so the girls had access and one from my bedroom. Weird remodelling project my father did,' he explained vaguely, and then yawned. 'Sorry. I didn't know you were in here.'

When he didn't move, she said forcefully, 'Well, would you mind leaving so I can finish getting dressed?'

'Uh…sure.' He spun around and went back the way he'd come. Annie stared at his retreating frame, her fingers itching to smooth themselves over his gorgeous naked torso. As he shut the door she forced herself to take a few deep breaths, knowing that without them there was no way she'd be able to finish dressing.

A minute later she was more suitably clothed and had combed her hair. She gathered up her belongings and knocked on the door Hayden had disappeared through. 'I'm finished,' she called, and waited for his reply. Nothing.

Slowly she opened the door and peered into his bedroom. He'd opened the curtains and sunlight seemed to be flooding in from all angles. He was lying on his stomach with his pillow over his head. Should she disturb him? If she didn't, he might think she was still using the bathroom.

'Hayden?'

He threw the pillow off and sat up in one swift motion. He stared at her, his eyes dark pools of desire. She felt her breath catch in her throat and tingles slide up and down her spine. Neither of them seemed capable of moving, both trapped by the invisible bonds which were binding them closer and closer together.

Annie's heart rate increased. Her lips parted to allow the rush of breath to escape. Her head started feeling light as she tried to hold firmly to reality. Say something, her brain demanded. She swallowed, slipped her tongue between her lips in order to help her throat and vocal cords to work smoothly. But as she was about to speak Hayden merely groaned and closed his eyes.

It was then Annie noticed his hands were clenched into tight fists, that every muscle in his body was taut, and she knew she either had to get out of there or do something to relax him.

She hesitated.

'Go, Annie,' he ground out between clenched teeth. 'Just go.'

Annie did as she was told and headed back into the bathroom, closing the door firmly behind her. She headed to the other door, fumbling with the lock but finally managing to get back to the safety of her room.

She dumped her PJs and towel onto the floor, burying her face in her hands, forcing herself to take deep, calming breaths. She shouldn't have come—was the first thought that entered her head. She shouldn't have allowed Hayden to bring her into the bosom of his family.

She shook her head, realising it wasn't a matter of should or shouldn't. She was *drawn* to Hayden. She *needed* to be near him. If he'd asked her to go to Timbuktu on a camel, wearing a superhero costume, she would have done so.

Her hands dropped back to her sides as she stalked over to the mirror. The eyes that looked back at her were wild with repressed passion, repressed hunger…and repressed love. How could she have been so careless?

Sure, she knew the infatuation had definitely started, but she'd thought she'd been able to control it—the long, painless slide into love. Now, though, it needed no more control, neither was it painless. She was already slap-bang in the middle of it and it was tearing her apart.

She was in love with Hayden Robinson.

The air in the room became more stifling than before and, after quickly pulling on her running shoes and hat, she lunged for the door. Quietly she opened it and peered around. The coast was clear. Silently she went down the stairs and was soon out the front door, trying not to sprint down the footpath.

By the time Annie returned an hour later, the house was well and truly awake. Hayden's mother was surprised she'd been out so early but then reminisced that Hayden was exactly the same. There was no sign of her son as Eloise ushered Annie into the kitchen.

'Sit down, dear, and let me get you some breakfast.'

'How's the bride this morning?' Annie asked politely.

'Jittery.' Eloise laughed. 'Just like her sisters were when

they got married. In honour of the occasion I'm making fresh pancakes, so how many would you like, dear?'

'One's fine, thank you.'

'There's also nice, warm croissants in that basket on the table. Help yourself.'

'Thank you.' The table had been set as though it were a restaurant.

'Coffee?' Eloise asked her.

'I'll get it, Mum.' Hayden walked into the room and kissed his mother's cheek. 'Good morning, mother of the bride.'

Eloise giggled and then sighed wistfully. 'This will be the last time I get called that. Mother of the bride.'

Hayden poured two cups of black coffee and carried them to the table. He sat down next to Annie and smiled. 'Just what you need. A nice, hot mug of *real* coffee.'

'Oh, you don't drink that instant stuff at home, do you, Annie?' Eloise asked in alarm.

'I'm afraid she does, Mum,' Hayden replied, and reached for a croissant.

'Well, buy her a real coffee-maker, Hayden...unless you're planning to share yours with her on a permanent basis?' Eloise looked so hopeful Annie almost laughed.

Hayden chuckled. 'Let's get Rowena's wedding out the way before you start planning mine.'

'Well, you didn't give me the opportunity to be the mother of the groom so why shouldn't I plan your wedding? Fancy eloping. Annie, don't you dare let him elope again or I won't be held responsible for my actions.'

'Did you enjoy your run?' Hayden asked, trying to deflect his mother.

He must have seen her leave the house. 'Ah...no. It was too humid to run and as I'd just had a shower...' She faltered, remembering the burning desire she'd seen in his eyes. By the look of him, he was remembering as well. Annie cleared her throat, conscious of the fact that Eloise was listening to their conversation. 'Uh...so I went for a walk. There's a nice little park down the road. Had a seat under a tree all to myself.'

'Yes, it *is* a lovely little park, dear.' Eloise chattered on about how her children used to play there when they were younger. 'Then there was the time Hayden broke his arm. How old were you, dear?'

'Fifteen.'

'I couldn't believe he'd been so careless.'

'What happened?' Annie smiled at him, delighted to watch him squirm a little.

'He fell out of a tree!' Eloise hooted with delight. 'Fifteen years old, had been climbing trees for years, and then—snap, the branch broke and down he came.' A call coming from upstairs had Eloise rushing out of the kitchen to see what was wrong.

Annie laughed. 'Don't be embarrassed. I broke my nose when I was fifteen.'

Hayden reached out and gently ran his finger down the small, bumpy contour of her nose. 'That's right. I remember you saying something about that before. How did it happen?'

'I was protecting Monty's honour.'

'Brenton?' Hayden smiled. 'I'd hardly think he'd need protecting.'

'Don't you believe it. He went to an exclusive boys' school and I went to the girls'. We had mixers every now and then and that's where we first met. There was nothing—no spark or anything—between us from the start and we became friends.'

Hayden had guessed as much and he was surprised at the relief he felt to hear her say it.

'Anyway, Valma Tucker, a…vindictive—for want of a better word—girl, started mouthing off about how Monty was trying to pressure her into sleeping with him. I was stunned and appalled so asked him straight out if it was true. He vehemently denied it. I then found out she was only trying to make her current boyfriend jealous. She was smearing my friend's reputation just to tug at the heartstrings of some bozo.

'It all came to a very exciting climax at one of the mixers where she spouted those rumours to a bunch of girls who were interested in Monty. Well, I'm sorry but I take my responsibility to my friends seriously and stood up for him.'

'What did you do?'

'I gave her a piece of my mind. She retaliated by connecting her fist with my nose.'

Hayden chuckled. 'Did you get into trouble?'

'Suspended for two weeks for fighting.'

'But *she* hit you.'

'She hit me *first*,' Annie replied.

Hayden let out a burst of his amazed laughter. 'You didn't.'

'I did. She had the biggest shiner of a black eye for weeks. It was worth it.'

'And Brenton? What did he do?'

Annie's smile mellowed. 'He's given me the gift of his unfailing friendship for the past twenty-five years.'

Hayden reached out and squeezed her hand. 'You're quite a woman, Annie Beresford.' Their gazes held and she sighed with longing. Hayden looked down at their hands before slowly pulling away. 'By the way, I've been meaning to ask you. Why do you call him Monty?'

'Brenton James Montague Worthington the third!'

'Ah.'

'He hates the name Montague so naturally, being the good friend that I am, I tease him about it.'

'Naturally.' Their eyes locked once more and the atmosphere intensified. 'Annie,' he whispered, and leaned a little closer.

The sound of Eloise coming back into the kitchen caused them to spring apart. The noise level increased with the arrival of Hayden's father, one of his sisters and two brothers-in-law. The moment had passed.

She had no idea what Hayden had told his family about

their relationship, but from the look of things, the two of them were almost engaged. Just the thought gave her heart palpitations and in the light of her new discovery that morning she desperately needed something to do.

Reaching across the table for the croissant basket, she inadvertently brushed her arm against Hayden's. Her breath caught in her throat and her gaze flew to his. 'Sorry,' she mumbled, and pulled back immediately. 'Uh…would you mind passing the croissants, please?'

Hayden reached out and passed her the basket, waiting while she took a croissant before replacing the basket in the middle of the table. He didn't look at her. He didn't say anything. He didn't smile.

Annie had an overwhelming urge to burst into tears. Instead, she concentrated hard on breaking her mouthwatering French roll into pieces. Moments later the rest of the clan, including the blushing bride, came into the kitchen for what Annie then learned was the traditional family breakfast before the wedding celebration.

Annie watched as Hayden joked freely with his sisters. The way he pulled funny faces at his two-year-old nephew and how he helped his mother in the kitchen. Throughout this, Annie only spoke when spoken to, not sure of the protocol for such a gathering.

They were amazing.

They all interacted with each other in such an easy, friendly manner. Hayden's father, Mike, was in a serious discussion with his son-in-law, Eloise was talking to her daughter's very pregnant 'bump' and the bride-to-be was laughing at her sister and brother-in-law.

They were something Annie had never had and what she yearned for with all her heart.

They were a family.

CHAPTER EIGHT

ANNIE felt a pang of longing wash over her and she looked away—right into Hayden's blue gaze. He had taken over the pancake flipping, and was watching her with concern. Her heart pounded wildly against her ribs and she forced a smile, swallowing over the lump of emotion in her throat.

The moment was broken when Katrina, the sister who was neither pregnant nor the bride-to-be, sat down beside her.

'Uh...will you quit making moon eyes at my brother and tell me about yourself?' she demanded.

'Excuse me?' Annie was a little taken aback.

Katrina sighed wistfully. 'I remember what it was like...being in love. Gazing across the crowded room into each other's eyes, wishing the family would just disappear so you could be alone.'

'Oh.' Annie laughed. 'That!'

'You're very quiet.'

'This is...a...new experience for me.'

'What? Breakfast?'

'A family breakfast.' Annie leaned a little closer. 'I have no siblings.'

'Oh.' Katrina's eyebrows hit her hairline and it was then Annie could see the resemblance between Hayden and his sister. 'No wonder you're so quiet. Never mind, you'll get used to it.'

'You get together often?'

'Usually every two months. This time, though, it's been less what with Christmas and New Year and now Rowena's wedding. So, how long have you and Hayden known each other?'

Annie smiled. 'Ah, I've heard about this.'

'What?'

'The sibling inquisition.'

Katrina laughed. 'I'm not letting you off the hook. We all have a lot of questions about you because until Hayden told Mum he was bringing a guest, we had no idea he'd been dating anyone.'

Annie wasn't sure what to say but decided that if he wasn't going to clue her in on things, she was just going to have to do something drastic…and tell the truth. 'We work together.'

'I knew that much. Things must have moved pretty quickly because he's only been in Geelong a short time, and when I visited him a few weeks ago he didn't say anything.'

'Ah, you're the sister who made the cinnamon rolls.'

'Yes,' Katrina said slowly, eyeing Annie more closely. 'I hope you enjoyed them.'

'I did.'

Katrina shook her head. 'Looks as though Hayden is moving *very* quickly. Then again, that's the way we Robinsons seem to be. Mum and Dad fell in love in under seven days. They hold the record. My husband and I were two weeks, Brigeeta was three weeks and I think Rowena was somewhere in between.'

Hayden must seem like a snail to the rest of his family, Annie thought. She glanced across but found his mother back in control of the pancakes. Quickly she looked around to find him coming up behind Katrina.

'What are you two talking about so cosily over here?'

'You,' his sister answered simply.

'Far be it from me to interrupt.' He turned his gaze to Annie. 'I have to go out for a while but I'll be back soon.'

'Uh…' Annie tried to stand but found her chair leg was jammed with the one beside her. She shifted again. 'Can I come with you? I have something I need to do.' Now was her opportunity to buy something to wear to the wedding.

'Stay. Enjoy the morning. Talk about me with my sisters. I know how girls love to do that.'

'That's mighty conceited of you,' she retorted, as she finally got the chairs untangled and stood.

'That's not what I meant.' He smiled at her. 'Girl talk.'

'As much as I'd like to, I *really* need to run an *important* errand.'

He placed both hands on her shoulders, stopping her from moving. 'Annie.' His tone was warm and encompassing and she felt as though he'd given her a big, secure hug. The touch of his hands on her shoulders caused her body to flood with tingles again, and the way he was looking at her made her mouth go dry. 'It's OK. Everything's under control.'

Before she could say or do anything, he dipped his head and brushed his lips across hers. 'I'll be back soon,' he said, and quickly left the room.

Annie couldn't have moved even if she'd wanted to. It was a second or two later that she realised all conversations, all the noise in the room had stopped—and everyone was looking at her.

Eloise had a strange misty look on her face. Katrina was nodding, as though in code, to her two sisters. Mike grinned widely. The moment seemed to last for ever and Annie wished, now more than ever, for a gigantic hole to open up and swallow her.

Instead, she decided to face the music. 'What?' she asked with a shrug of her shoulders.

'Nothing,' Brigeeta said, and conversations resumed.

'Have another cup of coffee, Annie,' Katrina said.

'No, thank you. I've eaten way too much food and drunk way too much coffee. Besides, I have something I need to do.'

'What?'

Annie shook her head, feeling embarrassed, and sank back down into her seat.

'What's wrong?'

Annie sighed, not used to confiding in people who were basically strangers. 'I forgot to get something to wear to the wedding,' she said softly.

'Really?'

'Work's been hectic.'

Katrina winked. 'I can imagine.'

'No. It really has,' Annie responded earnestly, not wanting Katrina to get the wrong impression.

'I was only teasing.' She drained her coffee-cup. 'Come on. Let's see what we can find.' She stood up. 'Ladies,' she announced to the room, 'we have an emergency.'

'Oh, no. I don't want to bother—' but Annie's pleas were cut short by Eloise, Brigeeta and Rowena as Katrina led her from the room. The hour that followed was something Annie had never experienced before. She tried on outfits offered by all four women, mixing and matching as best they could.

'I could just go and buy something,' she stated more than once.

'No, no, no.' Katrina waved the idea away as though it was preposterous. 'You don't want to spend all that money on one dress just for one day.' She continued to rummage through Rowena's closet. 'If only I'd known, I have a great dress that would look amazing on you. I could have packed it and brought it with me.'

'Me, too,' Brigeeta chimed in. 'In fact, most of my wardrobe doesn't fit me.' She patted her belly lovingly. 'You show so much earlier in your second pregnancy.'

'Just wait until your fourth,' Eloise said, and Brigeeta groaned. They continued to joke, enjoying the experience of having a real, live doll to dress up.

'Your hair is gorgeous,' Rowena enthused, flicking her straight, blonde hair over her shoulder. 'I'd give anything for mine to curl.'

'And your colour is so natural.' Brigeeta added. 'The style suits you.'

'Speaking of hair, aren't you supposed to be getting ready or something?' Annie asked Rowena.

'Not yet. Geeta will do my hair, Kat will do my make-up and Mum will help me dress. It's all organised.'

'OK.' Annie spun around in another dress she'd put on.

'The colour's not quite right for you.' Katrina said. 'Got any more, Ro?'

There was a knock at the door just as Rowena dived into the wardrobe once again. 'Come in,' one of the girls called.

'Is Annie in here?' Hayden asked, and when he spotted her, dressed in one of his sister's dresses, he frowned. 'Colour's not right.'

'That's what I said.' Katrina smiled.

'Mind if I borrow Annie?' Without giving her a chance to reply, he walked in, took her hand and started dragging her out of the room. 'Thanks for looking after her, girls.'

'Hayden?' He tugged her down the hallway and into the room she'd been given. Then he closed the door behind them. 'Hayden!'

'Shh. Close your eyes and hold out your arms.'

'What?'

'Do it,' he said softly. 'Please?'

She frowned, not quite sure, but nevertheless did as he'd asked. 'Keep them closed,' he warned, and she heard a door open.

'Hayden?'

'I'm still here. Keep them closed.'

'Fine.' She felt something heavy—a box—placed on her arms.

'Open sesame.'

Annie opened her eyes and stared down at a big, shiny, square box. 'Wha—'

'Happy birthday, Annie.'

Her jaw dropped open in amazement. 'How…how did you know it was my birthday?'

'Natasha told me. Open it.' He was eager to see her expression when she saw the present.

Annie slid the box onto the bed so she could lift off the lid. She gasped, her hand coming up to cover her mouth as she stared down at her present. Between the folds of white tissue paper was…a dress.

'Oh, Hayden.'

'Take it out,' he urged. 'Thank goodness Natasha also told me your size or this surprise would have been a nightmare.'

With trembling hands she lifted the dress out of the box and held it against her. It was sleeveless, made of raw silk and lined. A simple, fitted cut which would hug every curve of her body. The neckline was sheer from the bust up, leading to an elegant beaded collar. The hem came to mid-thigh…and the colour was a warm, russet-red.

'Oh, Hayden.' Tears welled in her eyes and she desperately tried to blink them away.

'Now, *that* colour suits you. But wait, there's more.'

He reached into the closet and pulled out another box. 'These are from the Worthington family. Natasha was most explicit in her instructions on what to buy to complement whatever dress I chose for you.'

Annie opened the second box, still unable to believe this was happening. It contained her accessories. Black shoes, an evening bag and a stole.

She laughed through her tears. 'Just like Natasha to be so bossy.'

'She was a fantastic help.'

'Hayden…I…' She trailed off and wiped away a tear. 'This is the nicest thing anyone has ever done for me.' She was thankful for her early morning revelation about being in love with him because now the feelings she felt for him had doubled in an instant. She gazed up at him, knowing the love she felt was reflected in her eyes.

'I wasn't sure what colour dress to get—' his tone was thick with raw emotion '—until I saw your underwear this morning. You looked…' He stopped and cleared his throat. 'Annie, I know you didn't want any kissing but I'm sorry…' His voice was soft but urgent as he covered the distance between them. 'I *have* to.'

He tenderly cupped her face, not wanting to crush the dress she still held in front of her, and brought his mouth possessively down on hers.

Annie couldn't help but put everything she was feeling— the desire, the passion and the love—into the kiss they shared. It was what she wanted as well, and she was glad he'd given in to the need to break the rules she'd set.

A few moments later Hayden pulled back and looked deep into her eyes. 'Time to get ready.' He stepped back and looked at the dress she still held up against her. 'I can't wait to see you in that.'

'I can't wait to put it on. Thank you.'

'My pleasure.' With that, he backed to the door, not taking his gaze off her until the last possible moment. After he'd gone, she hugged the dress tighter and whirled around the room, feeling every inch the birthday girl.

'I feel like Cinderella,' Annie whispered to Hayden, her hand resting on his arm as they walked into the church.

'I'm glad this place has air-conditioning,' he remarked.

Annie giggled. 'You're so romantic.' They were shown to their seats near the front on the bride's side and waited for the ceremony to begin. After Rowena's groom had come to stand at the front, they were all asked to be up-standing for the arrival of the bride. As the music started, Annie turned and looked down the aisle, waiting to catch a glimpse of Rowena.

She sighed with awe when she saw Hayden's beautiful sister start her journey up the aisle. 'She's breathtaking.' Annie glanced up at Hayden. It was then she realised he wasn't looking at Rowena. She followed his gaze and was stunned to see Adam standing three rows behind them.

Of course. Why hadn't she realised he'd be here? He was Rowena's cousin just as much as he was Hayden's. They were told to sit and she felt Hayden's arm slip firmly around her shoulders, drawing her closer. She relaxed against the warmth of his body and focused on Rowena.

His arm tightened possessively and the emotion surprised him. The need to protect Annie, to let every single man here—especially Adam—know that she was with him, became fierce. All he knew of her relationship with his cousin was that it was over. Did Annie have any old feelings left?

Jealousy rose, along with the urge to throw Annie over his shoulder and march out…but caveman tactics just weren't his style. He'd never met a woman who had made him feel this way, so…so…primitive. He shook his head slightly.

'Something wrong?' Annie whispered, concerned that he was shaking his head at a serious moment like this. Did he really hate the institution of marriage *that* much?

It was then Hayden realised his sister and new brother-in-law were in the process of exchanging their vows. He glanced down at Annie, surprised to see hurt in her eyes. She'd obviously thought he'd been shaking his head against what was happening at the front of the church.

He forced a smile and leaned closer. 'Everything's fine. Seems like yesterday she was just learning to walk.' He felt her relax once more and was glad he'd put her mind at ease. Focusing his attention on his sister, seeing the pure love shining in her eyes, he knew she'd be happy.

It appeared his sisters had better luck with love than he did. In fact, he couldn't recall Lonnie *ever* looking at him like that. He glanced down at Annie again and she turned her face up to his, her eyes glazed with unshed tears, her heart in her smile, and it was in that moment, that split second, Hayden realised he was in grave danger.

Two hours later they were dancing in the enormous marquee, Annie laughing at Hayden's ridiculous jokes.

'Here's one my five-year-old nephew told me. How do you know when an elephant's been in your fridge?'

'I have no idea.'

'The footprints in the butter.'

Annie chuckled at the ridiculousness of the joke. 'Of course.' She sighed. 'Hayden, I'm so happy. This is the best birthday ever.' She leaned up and kissed him. 'Thank you for making it so special.'

'I can't believe you weren't going to tell me. Fortieth birthdays should be cause for grand celebration.'

Annie looked around her. 'This *is* a grand celebration.'

'But it's not for you.'

Annie shrugged and smiled up at him. 'I have the only guest I need right here, in my arms.'

Hayden shook his head slowly. 'When you make comments like that, Annie, you only make it harder for me *not* to kiss you.'

'How about we lift that no-more-kissing rule, just for today, eh? After all, it *is* my birthday and, well, you've already broken the rule at least twice today, so…'

'So, I think that's a great idea,' he murmured, drawing her closer. He smiled down at her as she lifted her face. He saw impatience in her gaze and knew it matched his own. A tap on his shoulder jerked him out of the isolated world where only he and Annie existed, and he spun around, a scowl on his face. 'Adam.'

'Hi, Hayd. Mind if I cut in?'

'Yes, as a matter of fact, I do.' Hayden kept Annie firmly in his embrace, his anger and frustration aimed solely at his cousin, mounting steadily with each passing second.

'Hi, Annie. I was surprised to see you here.'

'Likewise,' she replied, relieved to find no twinges or pangs of regret as she spoke.

'Come on, cous. One little dance. I never pegged you as the possessive type.'

'It's all right, Hayden,' Annie said softly, giving his arm a little squeeze. 'It won't take long.'

Hayden stepped aside and reluctantly relinquished his hold on her. She smiled sweetly at him as he stepped off the makeshift dance floor.

'How's life, Adam?' she asked as they moved around

the floor, the correct distance—and a bit more—between them.

'Busy. You?'

'Same.'

'So you're with Hayden now,' he stated with a nod.

'Is that a problem?'

'No. No. So long as you're happy.'

'I am. *Very* happy,' she said sincerely.

'I can see it,' he mumbled reluctantly.

The atmosphere between them became stilted. 'Annie, I have something to say.'

She waited patiently.

'When I broke off our engagement, I wasn't entirely honest with you.'

'I know.'

'What?' He frowned.

'I know—about the other women,' she added.

'But—'

'I was about to break it off with you anyway, and not because of the other women. Well, they were part of it, I mean, but…' She stopped and took a breath. 'We weren't right for each other, Adam.'

'And Hayden is?'

'Yes. He is.' The words were stated with complete confidence. Regardless of what happened between herself and Hayden, he was definitely her one true love. 'And if you don't mind, I'm going to go to him now because he's just stormed outside.' She turned and made her way through the crowd with growing impatience, wishing they would simply part and let her through. Finally, she was outside and she scanned the area for Hayden. The gardens Rowena had hired for her wedding reception were lovely, but all Annie cared about at that moment was getting to Hayden.

She saw him disappear down a side path and hurried after him. 'Hayden.' He either hadn't heard her or was ignoring her. She pressed on, down the side path which ended in a T-junction. Which way had he gone? She looked both ways but couldn't see him.

'Hayden?' she called again, and as she listened, an intent look of disappointment on her face, she heard footsteps heading in her direction. She turned to come face to face with the man of her dreams. 'There you are.'

He didn't say anything, his face a mask.

'What's wrong?'

'Why did you dance with him?'

At least he wasn't going to beat about the bush. She smiled, knowing his directness was just one of the reasons why she loved him.

'He had things to say.'

'Such as?'

She took a deep breath. 'Such as he confessed to seeing other women while we were engaged.'

'You were engaged to him? You never told me that.'

She shrugged. 'Sorry. I didn't mean to conceal it from you. If you think about it, there are a lot of things we haven't talked about.'

Hayden knew she meant his ex-wife and his beautiful Liana. Right now, though, there was one question he needed to ask her, one he *desperately* needed to know the answer to, and he wasn't sure what her reaction would be. He took a deep breath. 'Do you still love him?'

'Adam?' She seemed surprised. 'No. Not at all.' It's you that I love, she added silently.

'You were shocked, in the church, when you first saw him. I thought that—'

'I was merely surprised, that's all. I honestly hadn't expected to see him. Hadn't even given him a thought.'

'Are you sure?'

'Yes.'

He took her hand and together they walked down the path, which skirted a pretty lake. 'My ex-wife did the same thing. Cheated on me, that is.'

Annie didn't say anything, didn't want to stop whatever

was in his heart from coming out, especially by saying the wrong thing. Instead, she squeezed his hand reassuringly.

'When she told me she was pregnant, I was hard pressed to believe it was mine, but she assured me it was.' He raked his hand through his hair and nodded. Slowly he extracted his wallet from his back pocket and retrieved a tatty old picture. He stared at it for a moment before holding it out to Annie.

'That's Liana.'

'Oh, Hayden, she's gorgeous.' Annie stared at the sleeping baby in the photo. She would have been only a few days old when it had been taken, wrapped up in a bunny blanket, her little fingers peaking over the edge.

'Yes. She was…amazing. I wasn't even sure I was ready to become a parent. We'd only been married a year,' he added, as though to justify his statement. 'I was working round the clock, doing my duty to provide for my wife, but an intern's salary isn't all that much.'

'I remember.' She handed the photo back. 'She looks…peaceful.'

Hayden stared at her. 'I thought that when I took it out just now. Strange, I haven't looked at that photo for so many years, but every other time I would think how alive she looked.'

'She still is alive, Hayden. She's alive in your heart.'

He was silent for a moment, there was just the sound of their footsteps on the footpath. 'Four weeks.' The two words were a whisper. He cleared his throat. 'Four glorious weeks I had of sheer happiness. I had no idea a baby would make me feel the way she did. She was helpless, completely dependent upon myself and Lonnie, yet I felt as though she'd given me a gift.'

'The gift of for ever?'

'Yes. Liana made me feel as though I could take on the world, that I could do no wrong in her eyes. I was her dad..for ever.'

Tears welled in Annie's eyes. 'You always will be.'

'I know.' He stopped walking and dropped her hand. He took out his wallet and put the picture back inside. 'After her death, life began to crumble.' He stared down at the ground. 'Lonnie blamed me entirely for Liana's death. I was a doctor. Why couldn't I resuscitate her? Why couldn't I fix the problem? How had she died?

'But with sudden infant death syndrome there aren't any clear answers. You wouldn't believe the things she accused me of.'

'She needed to blame…someone, anyone. It was easier than facing reality.'

He nodded at her words and looked into her eyes. The brown depths were filled with compassion. Usually he would brush other people's emotions aside in times like these. His parents, his sisters, they hardly spoke of Liana simply because they knew he didn't want their sympathy, but with Annie, for some reason he couldn't quite fathom, it was different.

'Then there's guilt. On top of my own guilt, Lonnie heaped hers. For two years we tried…well, *I* tried to patch things up. Nothing worked. She didn't want another child, well, not with me. The chasm between us had become so enormous it was too far for me to jump across. I threw myself into my work.'

Annie wasn't sure what to do. He was hurting so badly that she wanted to put a sticking plaster on his pain and kiss it better, just as he'd done with her knee. Instead, she flung her arms around his neck and pressed her lips to his own.

It wasn't a kiss of passion.

It wasn't a kiss of desire.

It was a kiss of love. Pure and simple… And one which he accepted.

CHAPTER NINE

'YOUR family are amazing,' Annie remarked to Hayden as she drove along the freeway, the Jaguar eating up the road with effortless ease. They'd not long passed through Albury/Wodonga and Annie was feeling comfortable behind the wheel. She laughed at the memory of his mother packing him a huge hamper of home-cooked food to take back with him. 'They're so...' she searched for the word she wanted '...familyish.'

Hayden chuckled as he rested his head back and closed his eyes. 'It was a good day.'

'I don't think Katrina's husband's going to sleep much—what with their seven-year-old daughter catching the bouquet.'

'Ah, she's gorgeous is my niece.'

'She'll break a lot of hearts when she's older.'

He chuckled again. 'I don't envy my brother-in-law *those* headaches.' He felt great. Since he'd spoken to Annie about Liana, he felt as though a weight had been lifted off his shoulders. She was a good listener and offered sound and logical advice when necessary. He valued her opinion, not only as a medical professional but as a friend.

'This has been so great—getting away this weekend,' she said jovially into the silence. 'Away from the hospital. Away from prying eyes and gossiping tongues.' Annie took a deep cleansing breath. 'Time to spend getting to know each other more.'

'Does this mean you're going to tell me about your family?'

She shrugged. 'There's nothing much to tell. I'm an only child. My dad has never loved me because I wasn't a boy

143

and my step-mother, who is fifteen years older than me, is only interested in his money.'

'And your mother?'

'She died when I was twenty. We weren't close.'

'They didn't try to have more children?'

'My mum miscarried with ten pregnancies after me. The doctors advised her to have a hysterectomy and that, as they say, was that.'

'Did your parents divorce?'

'No, but they weren't happily married either. After my mum died, my dad remarried within six months.'

'Any children there?'

'No. My step-mother went through IVF for years but in the end it all became too much for her and so they just stopped.'

'You would think all of this would make your father appreciate the child he has.'

'You would think that, but I wasn't the child he wanted. Big difference.'

A mobile phone beeped, indicating a text message. 'That's my phone,' Annie said. 'It's just inside my hand-bag, near the top, Hayden. Could you get it out and see who it's from?'

He felt a little self-conscious going through her bag, but did as he was asked. 'It's from Kelly.'

'Good.'

'She wants to know how much further we have to go.'

'Text her back and tell her we've just passed through Yackandandah.'

'How do you spell that?'

Annie laughed and helped him out.

Moments later, another text came through. ''Come directly to Bright hospital'',' Hayden read.

'Saddle up.' Annie concentrated on the winding road. All too soon, she was driving through the main street of Bright.

'That's where Kelly and Matt live,' she pointed out. 'Their clinic is across the road.'

'Handy.'

'This way to the hospital.' Another minute later, she'd parked the car outside the small district hospital and they quickly made their way inside.

'Thank God you're here,' Kelly said when she sighted them. Hayden reached out a hand to introduce himself but received a 'You must be Hayden' from the redhead in front of him.

'Correct.'

Kelly hefted a large emergency crate which was filled with medical equipment and motioned to the one next to her on the ground. 'Would you mind taking that, please, Hayden?' She walked off towards the car park. 'We've just had a call. There's been an accident at one of the vineyards on the road to Buckland. A couple of kids were playing around with tractors in a back paddock. Matt and Rhea, that's Matt's sister,' she explained for Hayden's benefit, 'have gone down to see what's happening. I'm expecting him to call through any moment now.'

She stopped by a four-wheel-drive and Annie quickly opened the tailgate. 'You've both just been drafted. Let's go.'

'What details do you have?' Hayden asked as Kelly drove.

'Two males, both around fifteen. Both tractors over-turned.'

'Races?' Annie asked.

'Either that or playing chicken,' Kelly replied disgust-edly. 'Parents heard a noise and went to investigate, then came back and raised the alarm. Both boys were reported unconscious and one was trapped—' Her mobile phone, sitting in a hands-free holder, rang and she leaned down and pressed a button. 'What's the news?' she asked.

Matt's voice came through. 'One trapped beneath the overturned cab of the tractor. Definitely fractured legs, pos-sible pelvis. Both still unconscious. Are you in the car?'

'Yes.'

'Annie and Hayden with you?'

'We're here, Matt,' Annie replied.

'Hey, mate. Sorry to do this to you.'

'Not a problem. Any fractures on the second boy?'

'Possible skull fracture. There's blood on a nearby rock as well as his head, so I'd say they've connected at some point. Left shoulder's badly banged up, too, but at least he was thrown clear. We'll need the SES boys to get this tractor off the first boy, though.'

'I'll call it in,' Kelly told her husband. 'Be with you in about fifteen minutes.'

'All right, honey. Drive safely.'

'I will,' she promised, love radiating through her tone before she disconnected the call. 'He's so cute,' she told them both. She contacted the SES and gave them the details before glancing at Annie in her rear-view mirror. 'So, let's do the social thing while we have a moment. How's Tash and Brenton?'

'Good.'

'The kids?'

'They had a stomach virus a week or so ago, then Natasha got it—'

'Then Annie got it,' Hayden interjected.

'Well, I hope you didn't bring it with you because none of us have had it.'

'No. I'm well and truly over it now.'

'Good to hear. How was the wedding?'

'It was lovely.'

'Oh, my gosh. I'm such a cad. Happy birthday for yesterday, Annie. Sorry, this emergency has thrown everything out, but we have a cake and everything back home so, regardless of how long this emergency takes, you're just going to have to stay and eat a piece.'

'If you insist.'

'I do. So the wedding was lovely? What did you end up wearing?'

Annie glanced at Hayden who was sitting in the front

seat next to Kelly. Annie had insisted he sit in the front because he had longer legs and needed the room. 'Well…Hayden actually bought me the most gorgeous dress as my birthday present. It's just…stunning. I felt like a princess when I was wearing it.'

Kelly turned to look at Hayden and he felt himself squirm a little. 'Natasha said I'd like you. Just keep being nice to our Annie and you'll do just fine, Professor.'

'Kelly has a strong Irish streak running through her. Don't be too alarmed by it,' Annie said.

'You seem to know quite a lot about me,' Hayden remarked.

'I should hope so. We're all very possessive of our darling friend, aren't we, Annie? But if you think *I'm* bad…' She laughed. 'Just wait until you meet my sister-in-law.'

As they neared the accident site, the talk turned to the different scenarios they might find. By the time Kelly stopped the vehicle, everyone was ready for duty.

'We've set up drips to stabilise them. The boy beneath the tractor, Gordon, has regained consciousness once or twice but he's slipping in and out. He's had morphine for the pain. Obs are stable. The second boy, Leo, is still out. His obs aren't so good but I've called through to Wangaratta hospital and they're sending an ambulance. Should be here in around twenty-five to thirty minutes. Rhea's keeping a close eye on him.' Hayden and Annie had helped Kelly unload the equipment and were pulling on gloves while Matt had been talking.

'How are the parents holding up?' Kelly asked.

'Not too good, as you can imagine.'

'I'll talk to them,' Kelly offered.

Annie walked across to where Gordon was, glad they still had about three hours left of light so she could see the undulating surface of the ground. 'Gordon?' she called as she checked his pupils. 'My name's Annie.'

'I'm Hayden. Gordon, can you hear us?'

No response.

'Pupils equal and reacting to light.'

'Pulse isn't settling down as much as I'd hoped,' Matt commented.

'BP is still quite low,' Hayden said, after releasing the pressure on the sphygmomanometer. 'If the femoral arteries have been severed, he'll bleed to death if we don't get him out a.s.a.p.'

'We need to stabilise him, and fast,' Annie agreed. She lay down on the ground and peered beneath the tractor to where Gordon's legs were. 'How long until the SES get here?'

'I'll check,' Matt replied, and pulled out his mobile.

'Let's get a blood transfusion going, stat,' Hayden said and they worked together, quickly setting up the unit of blood expander Kelly had brought with her from the hospital.

'SES ETA—ten minutes.'

'Good. Once the tractor's off him, we're going to have to move fast.' Hayden and Annie discussed with Matt and Kelly the surgery they'd need to do. 'We'll need to repair those arteries immediately.'

'They've already done enough damage,' Kelly agreed.

'I gather the staff at the hospital are organised?' Hayden asked.

'I called the anaesthetist in just before you arrived,' Kelly confirmed.

Leaving Hayden to monitor Gordon, Annie went across to see how Rhea was getting on with Leo.

'Howdy, stranger,' Rhea said.

'Hi. How's he doing?'

'He's stable but he'll definitely need a headscan.' Rhea spoke softly so as not to panic Leo's mother, who was close by talking to Kelly.

'The concussion's that bad?' Annie asked, and after she'd changed her gloves, she felt Leo's scalp. 'Definite skull fracture.'

'Ribs are fractured as well.'

Annie carefully felt around the front of Leo's ribs. 'Right T5 and 6 feel broken. Left T4, 5 and 6 don't feel good,' she remarked, as she tried to feel, but with the way Leo was lying, ensuring his airways were clear and accessible, she couldn't tell for sure. 'Let's get another bag of saline going.'

With the sound of approaching vehicles, Annie sent up a silent prayer of thanks. That would be the SES crew. The sooner they had that wreck off Gordon the better. Matt gave the commands for the SES workers and about fifteen minutes later they were able to carefully move Gordon out from beneath.

'It's worse than I thought,' Hayden mumbled to Annie as the stretcher was manoeuvred into the back of the SES vehicle, which was decked out to handle a medical stretcher. Gordon's mother was now crying hysterically and Kelly was doing her best to calm the situation.

'At least he's in better shape to be anaesthetised than he was an hour ago,' Annie added.

'True. I think he'll need to go to Melbourne for micro-surgery.'

'Let's get him back to Bright hospital first.' One of the SES workers drove them back to the hospital, passing the ambulance from Wangaratta on their way. 'At least we know Leo will soon be on his way,' she murmured.

Pulling into the hospital car park, two staff members helped them get Gordon inside. Hayden and Annie introduced themselves to the anaesthetist and the rest of the staff as they hurried towards Theatre.

Hayden gave a brief summary of Gordon's situation, letting the anaesthetist know Matt had administered morphine before the anaesthetist set to work. Annie and Hayden scrubbed side by side, talking over techniques and possibilities.

'He'll need to be transferred to Melbourne once he's stabilised,' Hayden told the theatre sister. 'Let's get to work Dr Beresford.'

Gordon's legs were in a bad way and their initial guess that the femoral artery in each leg had been damaged was confirmed. Hayden repaired them before calling for X-rays. As this was a small hospital, they didn't have a portable machine, so Gordon was wheeled over to another room for the radiographs to be taken.

'Three-dimensional scans would be preferable,' he mumbled, as he held the processed film up to the light. 'But for now these will do just fine.'

After the theatre was set up again, and Annie and Hayden had scrubbed once more, they set to work. With the femur being a long bone, there were several pieces which had been badly crushed beneath the tractor.

'What I wouldn't give for a vascular surgeon on tap,' Annie said. She shook her head as they debrided the wound and stabilised the fracture with a G. and K. nail, as well as fixing the smaller fragments of bone back into place with wires, plates and screws. 'It's like a jig-saw puzzle.'

Once one leg was done, they started on the other. Both the tibia and fibula in Gordon's left leg were also badly broken, but amazingly the lower bones of his right leg weren't as severely damaged.

Kelly came into Theatre and was able to assist, reporting that Leo had been transferred to Wangaratta hospital and was being seen by both the neuro and spinal surgeons.

'How are their parents?'

'Gordon's mother is in the waiting room and has settled down. Rhea's gone to Wangaratta with Leo's parents, and Matt's stayed to help the SES guys get everything sorted out.'

'What about the police?' Hayden asked as they continued with their work.

'Joe—that's Rhea's husband—is on his way out there now. He just had to wait for my in-laws to get back from their trip to Wodonga before he could leave the children. I'm not complaining because he was minding my children as well as his own.'

When the operation was over, Annie sat down in the small kitchenette and put her feet up on the chair opposite. The sun had well and truly set but at least Gordon was in a better position for recovery. When she'd first seen the damage to his left leg in particular, she'd been appalled. In fact, she'd wondered whether she and Hayden could actually save the leg, it was that bad. Thankfully, though, with Kelly's assistance, Gordon was definitely doing much better.

'Tired?' Hayden asked as he sat down beside her, putting his feet up on the same chair as hers.

'Exhausted, but feeling good.'

'Me, too.' He took her hand in his, turning it over as though he was searching carefully for something. He frowned in concentration and Annie felt a sense of foreboding. 'You make me think, Annie.' The words were said slowly and carefully. 'You make me *feel*—and that's something I haven't honestly allowed myself to do for years with anyone not directly related to me.'

'Ready for your party?' Kelly bounced into the room, her tight red curls springing everywhere. Hayden dropped Annie's hand and stood up, walking over to the bench. 'The kids have decorated the house just for you, Annie, so dredge up some energy from somewhere and let's get moving. Your patient is stable and, apart from some paperwork to cover the fact that you've operated as visiting surgeons at our hospital, you're all done here.' When neither of them moved, she added temptingly, 'We have real coffee ready and waiting at home.'

Hayden turned and smiled at her. 'Well, why didn't you say so? Come on, Annie. Up and at 'em.'

As Hayden drove his Jaguar to Kelly's and Matt's house, Annie glanced surreptitiously at him, wondering if he was going to continue with their earlier conversation. She made him feel. Well, surely that was a good thing, wasn't it?

The problem was that the drive from the hospital to her friends' house was over and done with in a matter of minutes and soon they were inside, Annie being enveloped by the excited children. They all sang a rousing chorus of 'Happy Birthday', making Annie feel very loved and very special.

'Blow out your candles, Annie,' Lisa, Kelly's eldest, squealed excitedly. 'I counted them myself. There's forty candles on there and they're all just for you.'

Hayden laughed beside her and she turned to glare at him. 'What are you laughing at? Hmm? You're already forty.'

'Forty-one,' he clarified.

'Well, there you go so keep quiet, old man.' She turned her attention back to the abundant blaze before her. 'I think I'm going to need some help.'

'Great,' Matt muttered good-naturedly. 'Cake with spit.'

With help from the children around her, Annie blew out the candles on her cake, and when the little wax sticks had been removed, she laughed. 'I don't think there's a part of this cake that doesn't have a hole in it.'

An hour later fatigue was definitely starting to set in and she sat back in her chair and yawned.

'Why don't you stay the night?' Kelly offered.

Annie smiled but shook her head. 'We have a pelvic fracture operation tomorrow so we'd better get back.'

'I like him, Annie.'

'But?' Annie could tell Kelly had something more to add.

'But he seems to have a lot of issues to work through.'

'He does.' She watched Hayden talking to Matt on the other side of the room, glad both men were getting along.

'I just don't want to see you hurt again.'

'It's too late,' Annie whispered.

Kelly gasped. 'You're in love with him?'

Annie nodded. 'So, in fighting for Hayden, I have everything to gain and everything to lose.'

Kelly smiled at her friend. 'True love *always* triumphs in the end.'

'I sincerely hope so.'

During their late evening drive from Bright back to Geelong, Hayden didn't say anything personal relating to himself or Annie. She forced herself to ignore it, thinking that surely it was a good thing she had made him *feel* again.

Instead, they talked quietly about an eclectic range of topics, enjoying the opinions expressed and once or twice agreeing to disagree. When they arrived back at their apartments Hayden stood like a statue outside his door, and after a brief pause offered Annie his hand.

Slowly, she placed hers in his and stared into his mesmerising blue eyes. 'Thank you for a lovely weekend, Hayden.'

'Thank you for protecting me from my family.'

She laughed. 'I seriously doubt you needed protecting at all. Personally, I think you had a lot of unanswered questions about me, and that was your main motive for inviting me.'

Hayden smiled. 'You *did* protect me, believe me you did.'

But at what cost? she thought, her heart bubbling over with love for him. 'If you ever need protecting again…' She took a small step closer, the atmosphere between them changing in that one instant. 'You know where to find me.'

Hayden slowly nodded his head. With a muffled groan he tugged her into his embrace. His arms enfolded her to him and he bent his head to kiss her. His mouth was hungry and possessive against her own and she welcomed the invasion, desperately hoping he'd feel how much he meant to her.

She put everything into this kiss, knowing it would have to last her for quite a while. The closer they'd got to Geelong, the faster he'd started to withdraw. The weekend was over and it was definitely time to get back to reality. The problem Annie faced was that *he* was her reality.

His happiness, his tenderness, his vulnerability. Everything about Hayden was very real to her, and the more she got to know him, the stronger her love became. She was starting to need him the same way she needed air to breathe. Never had she felt this way. Never in all her forty years had she felt such an all-encompassing, soul-consuming love as she did for Hayden.

She threaded her fingers through his hair, holding his head firmly in place, never wanting him to leave her. The touch of his warm hands on her back, the way his thumbs moved in little circles, enticing her, bringing her entire body to life, were enough to make her forget all her sensibilities and throw caution to the wind.

Her body was on fire and as he groaned with agonising passion against her mouth, she knew he felt the same way.

'How?' He broke free and held her, placing small kisses against her neck. 'How is it possible you make me forget myself? I can't seem to get enough of you, Annie. No matter how many times I tell myself I'm never touching you again, I just can't seem to stick to it.'

His breathing was harsh, his words raspy with desire. 'I want you, Annie. So much that it's starting to affect my logical reasoning.'

Annie couldn't help it. A bubble of laughter rose up and she wasn't able to clamp down on it. 'Heaven forbid I interfere with your logical reasoning,' she teased.

Hayden pulled back to look at her, desire still smouldering in his eyes. She reached up and kissed him on the lips. 'You really know how to sweep a girl off her feet with pretty words.'

'You're laughing at me?'

'No, Hayden. I'm laughing at the situation.' She smoothed his hair back with her fingers. 'You're such a thoughtful man and I can see how you'd be struggling at the moment to try and figure out exactly what it is you feel for me. You like me, you want me…you need me.' She knew she was pressing him but the time felt right and she'd learnt the hard way to follow her instincts so there was no way she was ignoring it this time around. Her future happiness depended on it.

'The problem is that you need to have your emotions wrapped up into a nice little bundle with a label on it, and that's understandable because you've been hurt in the past. So have I, but this time, Hayden, this time you need to let them flow.'

'Why?'

He was withdrawing. If not physically, then mentally.

'Because otherwise you risk lying to yourself.' Annie broke the contact first and stepped away from him. 'You were so relaxed in Sydney, more…yourself.'

Hayden took two steps back and shoved his hand impatiently through his hair. 'I was allowed to kiss you in Sydney.'

Annie laughed. 'True.' She took a deep breath and plunged in. 'So why don't we try it?'

'What? Kissing?'

'Dating,' she replied patiently. 'That way you can kiss me whenever you like.'

Hayden took a deep breath and slowly exhaled. 'Dating.' He nodded. 'You're right. It would have its benefits…'

'But?' she prompted.

'I don't know, Annie. I don't know whether I'm up or down, hot or cold. You've…you've turned my life upside down and inside out and I…' He placed his hands on his hips. 'I didn't ask for that.'

'Neither did I.'

Hayden looked over his shoulder, as though realising they were still standing in the corridor outside their apartments. 'I don't think this is the time or the place,' he mumbled, picking up his bag.

'OK.' She'd lost him. She swallowed over the lump in her throat and dug deep in her handbag for her keys. 'Sleep well and I'll…' She glanced down, desperate to get control over her emotions. 'I'll see you tomorrow.' She forced a smile and, after finding her keys, unlocked her door, hefted up her bag and walked through. Instinct made her turn to see Hayden still standing in the corridor, watching her. 'I had a really great time and thank you again for my birthday present.' With that, she closed the door.

She leaned against it, fantasizing he would come to her, but even before she heard the sounds of him moving about in his apartment, she knew it was almost over. She hoped the pain would be swift and of short duration but look where hope had got her so far.

On wooden legs she walked to the phone and sat down in a chair while punching in Natasha's phone number.

'Sorry to call so late,' she said, when her friend picked up the phone.

'That's OK, I was expecting it. Kelly called and told me about the emergency.'

'Oh.'

'She also told me you've fallen in love with Hayden.'

'Yup.' Annie closed her eyes, feeling the tears well up. 'How stupid was that.'

Natasha's chuckle turned into a sigh. 'Pretty stupid, but take heart, Annie. It happens to the best of us.' They talked a bit more about the weekend before Natasha asked, 'So what's next?'

'I honestly don't know.' Annie's breath hiccuped as she breathed in. 'OK. I'm going to go to bed now.'

'Hang in there, sweetie. Remember—we love you.'

Annie rang off but stayed where she was, unable to force her dejected body to move. He couldn't kiss her like that and not *feel* anything—could he? He'd said that she made him feel, so she'd be almost willing to bet that he was either in the process of falling in love with her or, like herself, was already there.

How? How could she convince him this was the real deal and it was worth taking a chance? Forcing her legs to move, she picked up her bag and took it into her room. She unpacked, checking pockets for tissues and bits of paper before putting her clothes in the laundry basket.

If it turned out that Hayden wouldn't come around, she had to have a plan to save her heart. She would have to transfer from the hospital because there was no way she could cope with working with him everyday, loving him as she did. She would have to find a different place to live because there was no way she could cope with living next door to him, loving him as she did.

She would pick up the pieces of her life, she would rely on her close friends to see her through and she would not only survive without him but she would succeed.

She *had* to. She just *had* to.

Otherwise…she was afraid she'd shrivel up and die inside.

He needed to concentrate.

He was due to be in Theatre fixing Mr Bouchard's pelvic fracture with Annie standing across the table from him for the next four hours and he needed to concentrate. Yet every time he saw her, every time she looked at him, every time she walked by, her perfume would linger and entwine itself around him so completely he had trouble breathing.

'You all right?'

Hayden's eyes snapped open and he glanced at the woman who had put him in this quandary in the first place. 'Yes.'

'Didn't sleep well?'

'No.' He continued scrubbing his hands and arms, preparing for the operation. How could he possibly escape Annie when he was so conscious of everything she did? They needed to talk. They needed to sort things out, but now was definitely not the time.

'OK. I'm done.' She elbowed off the taps and turned to the scrub nurse who would help her gown. The two women chatted idly while Hayden finished scrubbing. Annie appeared to be in good spirits so she obviously didn't harbour any grudges against what he'd said…or more correctly *hadn't* said last night.

She was different, *really* different from the women he'd dated in the past—and the opposite of Lonnie, which he'd soon come to realise. Now…Annie wanted to be with him. His first thought had been to jump at the chance. To be able to spend time with her without having to think up an excuse first. To be able to continue their amazing conversations. To be able to take her in his arms and kiss her.. any time he felt like it. Yes, he wanted to date her. Of course he wanted to date her, but he knew where she wanted it to end, and *that* was the problem.

He frowned, forcing all thoughts of Annie to the back of his mind. He shoved them into a box and firmly shut the lid. Compartmentalised. He walked into Theatre with the pelvic fracture surgery firmly in mind.

'Could I have the X-rays up?' he snapped, surprising more than the sister he spoke to.

'Certainly, Hayden.'

He studied them before walking to the table. He got the nod from the anaesthetist and addressed his staff. 'Mr Bouchard, a thirty-two-year-old male, received several fractures, including a left innominate and acetabular fracture, which is what we're going to concentrate on today. I'll be using open reduction and internal fixation, using two separate approaches—Kocher-Langebeck and ilio-inguinal. This will ensure we fix both the anterior and posterior bones of the pelvis. As none of you have performed this particular operation with me before, I suggest that if you have any questions, you ask instead of guessing.'

He forced his gaze to meet Annie's. 'I'm presuming you've assisted with pelvic fractures before?'

'Yes, but feel free to talk me through it if you'd prefer.'

She was all business and he was glad to see it. It helped him keep everything in focus. 'Right. I'll be making an incision along the anterior two thirds of the iliac crest, continuing down to the midline only two fingerbreadths above the symphysis pubis.' He held out his hand. 'Scalpel.'

'Scalpel,' Annie repeated as she firmly placed the instrument into Hayden's outstretched hand.

The anterior abdominal muscles were also incised from the iliac origin and the fracture exposed. 'Stabilising with a three-hole plate and two-millimetre screws.' Hayden held out his hand for the drill.

Once the fracture had been stabilised on the anterior side, the posterior approach was next. Hayden made another incision approximately sixteen centimetres along the proximal side of the femur toward the greater trochanter, angling slightly posteriorly to the iliac crest.

They fixed the fracture with one posterior interfragmentary screw and a small pelvic reconstruction plate.

'Check X-ray, then close.' He stepped away from the table as the portable X-ray machine was wheeled over. He much preferred the large hospitals where everything was on hand—the staff, the equipment. He thought about the surgery they'd performed in Bright yesterday—it seemed so long ago—and he had to admit he'd been a little worried about whether they'd be able to save the leg or not. Thankfully, they'd had a positive ending.

Hayden glanced at Annie. She was happy today. Smiling, laughing—the way she'd been on Saturday. Saturday—her birthday. She'd made him promise not to tell his mother or his sisters that it had been her birthday because she hadn't wanted any fuss made.

'It's Rowena's day,' she'd told him firmly.

He watched her now, on the other side of the room, talking with the theatre sister, and the primal urge to stalk over there, rip off her mask and press his lips to hers was extremely hard to control. That would *definitely* get the tongues wagging in the hospital, but as quickly as the impulse came he squashed it.

Annie wanted marriage. Not only marriage but marriage *and* children. He shook his head. Dating her would have so many benefits—short-term benefits—but in the end he'd break her heart, and probably his own in the process.

He could feel himself falling for her—bigger, brighter and far better than anything he'd ever felt for Lonnie. Lonnie had been a mere infatuation compared to Annie. She was the real thing. If he left now, they'd both be in one piece, able to survive. If he dated her and *then* left… He shuddered. It wasn't worth contemplating.

'X-rays are ready, Hayden.'

He shoved his thoughts of Annie out of his mind again, determined she would stay there until the end of this operation. 'On screen.' He peered at the fracture sites and, well pleased with his handiwork, announced it was time to close. It would take at least half an hour to close in layers and then staple the large incisions but then he would be free of Annie for the rest of the day.

After the theatre session with Mr Bouchard, Annie finished off some paperwork, did a quick ward round and, as it was now almost eight o'clock in the evening, decided to head home. She packed some work to take with her, and as she came to the end of the ward, she looked down the corridor to where Hayden's office was situated.

Was he there?

Knowing they needed to talk, she headed towards his office. She knew, even before she reached his door, that he would be in there. Of course he would be—he was avoiding her. She knocked and, without waiting for an answer, walked in. He looked up from the paperwork he was doing.

'I knew I'd find you here.' She smiled brightly, noting the look of pleasure, then pain, that quickly filtered across his face before being replaced by a non-emotional mask. 'Doesn't it seem like an age since we were in Sydney, rather than just yesterday?'

'Yes,' was all the reply she received. He put his pen down and leaned back in his chair. 'Something wrong?'

'With the patients? No, everything's fine.' She put her briefcase and handbag on the floor and sat in the chair opposite his desk.

'What's on your mind?' He stretched his arms up and twisted his shoulders.

'You.'

He stopped still before dropping his arms and getting to his feet. He started to pace the room and Annie tried to hide her smile. He was so adorable when he was agitated.

'Annie…' He stopped on the other side of the room and looked at her.

'Hayden.'

He raked a hand through his hair and exhaled deeply. 'This isn't going to work.'

'What?' she asked innocently, knowing all along exactly what he was referring to.

'Us. Dating. Seeing each other.'

'And why not? Aren't you attracted to me?'

'You know I am. That's part of the problem.'

Annie stood and walked towards him, slowly but with a firmness in her step. She stood before him and placed one hand on her heart and one on his. He was warm and alive beneath her touch and a shiver of anticipation burst through her. 'Feel. Feel what you do to me. Feel what I do to you. This can't be wrong, Hayden, because it feels so right. It *is* so right. I know this because…' This was her moment of truth. She knew how he would react but she also knew that she *had* to tell him. 'Because I've fallen in love with you.'

Hayden didn't move.

His gaze was transfixed with hers and in that instant she felt the most complete connection with him. Slowly she placed her other hand on his chest before sliding both up and over his gorgeous broad shoulders. He was tense and she couldn't blame him. Still, she could no more stop what she was doing now than she could stop falling in love with him.

Taking a small step, bringing their bodies into contact, she slid her hands around his neck, urging his head closer.

'Can't you feel my heart beating wildly?' she whispered. 'It beats for you and you alone, Hayden.'

His gaze flicked between her eyes and her mouth, reading the message of love in her brown depths and wanting the feel of her luscious pink lips on his own. He couldn't believe it. *Annie loved him.* The knowledge was enough to make him want to whoop for joy, as well as run as fast as he could in the opposite direction.

He swallowed roughly and almost crumpled to the floor when she pressed her lips to his neck. Groaning with desire, Hayden dragged her body close, wrapping his arms about her.

'Annie.' Her name was thick with repressed passion and she loved the way it sounded coming from his lips. Turning her head, their lips met as though programmed to find each other under any circumstances.

Annie put everything she felt, everything from the depths of her soul into the kiss to show him just how much he had come to mean to her during the past few weeks. If he doubted her verbal declaration of love, surely this must convince him she was sincere.

He wanted her. His possessive mouth moved over hers, taking from her everything she was willing to give. He was selfish, he knew it, but he also knew he couldn't help it. Annie was special. She was an incredible woman and one, he was sure, he would never grow tired of…and therein lay the problem.

A few ragged moments later Hayden forced his mouth from hers.

'Hayden?'

'Shh.' Both were breathing hard. 'Just let me hold you.' Although that was his intention, her scent wound itself about him, making his head feel as though it were full of cotton wool. He was incapable of coherent thought where it pertained to Annie and how perfect she felt in his arms. He kissed her neck, her cheeks, her eyelids and finally her mouth once more, unable to resist her allurements.

He groaned again and with superhuman effort gently put her from him, his lips still pressed on hers until the arms' length distance was too far for him to physically continue to kiss her.

'We can't.'

'Hmm?' Annie gazed up at him, her eyes filled with love. Why hadn't he seen it before? He should never have taken her to Sydney with him… But he'd been unable to control the need to have her close, just as he'd been unable to stop himself from kissing her just now.

'We can't,' he said more forcefully, and walked back to his desk. 'Can't you see? I'd break your heart.'

'It's too late, Hayden.'

Guilt swamped him.

'It's also not your fault,' she replied. She took a deep breath and forced her legs to work. Putting one foot in front of the other, she walked back to the chair opposite his desk and sat. It was either that or fall down in a heap on the floor. Then again, wouldn't that require him to help her up? He was her knight in shining armour after all. It would also be another excuse to have his arms around her. She giggled, dismayed with herself for not being a practised damsel in distress.

'I'm a grown woman and I choose who I give my heart to. I love you. There's no two ways about it and I will love you for the rest of my life.'

'But you want to get married!' His tone was insistent. 'Have children!'

'That's right.'

'Marriage isn't me, Annie. I've been there. I've tried it and I've failed. My actions, my whole being was responsible for ruining three people's lives. Mine, Lonnie's and my daughter's. I won't be held responsible for ruining yours as well.'

'So this is the reason you won't date me,' she stated logically. 'Because I want to get married and you think you'll ruin my life.'

'Yes. Annie I'm sor—'

She held up her hand. 'No, don't. Please, don't.' After taking a deep, cleansing breath, she stood, glad her body was co-operating. She picked up her briefcase and handbag before walking around his desk and standing on tiptoe. 'Goodbye, Hayden.' She pressed a brief kiss on his lips then turned and walked out the door.

It was over.

CHAPTER TEN

HAYDEN had rostered Annie on call for nights, probably thinking it would make life easier for both of them. In some ways it did as she threw herself into her work, but when she saw him in clinics and ward rounds it was like having a little glimpse of paradise.

'It's like wanting a calorie-filled piece of cake, knowing you're going to get indigestion from it and then living with it on your hips for the rest of your life. And for what?' she asked Natasha and Katrina.

'For *love*!' both women replied.

It had been a whole week since the scene in Hayden's office and Katrina, who had called Annie several times on her return to Melbourne, decided she needed 'cake' therapy. Annie happened to mention this to Natasha who'd completely agreed, and so her two friends had kidnapped her, forcing her to spend the day with them at Acland Street in Melbourne which was renowned for its amazing cakes.

Annie took a sip of her coffee and pushed the irresistible mud cake away.

'He's hardly sleeping.' Katrina informed her, pushing the plate back in front of her. 'He's so torn apart, Annie, it's killing him.'

Annie looked at one friend, then the other through shimmering tears. 'I miss him.'

'Of course you do.' Natasha squeezed her hand reassuringly.

Annie sniffed and dug around in her bag for a tissue. 'It hit me when I saw him yesterday. He was talking to Brenton and the two of them were laughing, and I was so happy that he was getting to know the people I consider family and also the fact that they like him and it hurts so much. I just wanted to throw myself into his arms and tell him to accept fate.'

'He probably would have appreciated it.' Katrina laughed. 'He's being sanctimonious and stubborn. He's also deluding himself if he thinks his love for you is going to disappear simply because he doesn't see you.'

'Absence makes the heart grow fonder,' Natasha recited.

Annie blew her nose and had more of her cake, savouring the taste. 'I need to talk to him again.'

'And say what?'

Annie closed her eyes and shook her head. 'Good question.' She sighed dejectedly. 'It's just that I don't think he's made the right decision. Not for me, not for him.'

'So?' Natasha asked. 'What are you going to do about it?'

Annie straighted in her chair and lifted her chin defiantly. 'I'm going to fight for him.'

'Atta girl.'

'I'm going to ask him out on a date and *show* him that we belong together. I know he's worried he's going to mess up my life, the way he thinks he messed up in the past, but I need to convince him he's wrong.'

'He won't be able to resist you.' Katrina leaned forward in her chair, a bright grin on her face. 'Where are you going to take him? Secluded restaurant? Ooh, I know, a walk along the beach at sunset. How romantic.'

'You could cook dinner for him in your apartment,' Natasha suggested.

'Yes, nice and intimate.' Katrina nodded her approval.

Annie shook her head. 'I know *exactly* where I'm going to take him.'

'Where?' they both asked.

'To the pool hall.'

'What?' Katrina was appalled. Natasha just laughed.

Annie didn't care. Her brain was working nine to the dozen, going over everything she'd need to do. 'I just can't do it while I'm working nights. How am I going to convince Wesley to swap a shift with me?'

'*Please*, Wesley?' Annie begged the next day. She'd stayed longer at the hospital specifically to catch up with her colleague. 'It's just one shift. One little night duty, that's all.' Remembering the hospital grapevine already had herself and Hayden paired off as a couple, she continued, 'It's been so hard lately, what with me doing nights. Hayden and I have hardly seen each other.'

'Talk to him. He's the one who draws up the rosters.'

'I know, but someone has to do nights and he can't show favouritism just because we're going out. He wants to be fair.'

Wesley thought this over for a long minute. 'I want double the usual payment you give to everyone else.'

'Payment?' Annie frowned and then realisation dawned. 'Chocolate frogs? Sure. You can even have triple if you like.'

'Deal.' Wesley held out his hand and they shook on it.

'Thank you. I'll go and get the payment right now.' Just in case he changed his mind, she thought as she rushed to the small shop, determined to buy all the chocolate frogs in stock.

She'd just finished paying for one large box of fifty chocky frogs when she turned and collided with Hayden. His arms came about her and her breath caught in her throat. She gazed up into his eyes, drowning in the beautiful blue depths, unable to break away.

Hayden seemed affected by their natural chemistry as well. Was that her heart beating out such a wild tattooing rhythm or was it his? Annie couldn't tell. She wanted nothing more than for him to haul her into his arms and place his mouth possessively over her own. She forced herself to look away and it was then she realised they were the centre of attention of most of the staff in the small shop.

Hayden must have realised it, too, because he took a step

away and forced a smile. 'I'm surprised to see you still here. I thought you'd be tucked up in bed by now.' Why on earth had he said that? It was the thought of Annie in her bed that kept him awake most nights. He searched earnestly for something else to say. It was then he noted the box of chocolate frogs.

'Stocking up?'

'Huh?'

He pointed to the box.

'Oh, no. Payment for…a favour.'

'Must be a big favour.'

She nodded slowly. 'It was…is. Listen, Hayden, are you free tomorrow night?' She knew he wasn't working because she'd checked the roster. Wednesday night was free all around, especially as Wesley had agreed to do her on-call duty!

'Uh…' He hesitated, not sure what to say.

'Just a game of pool. That's all.' She tried not to sigh with longing as she breathed in his scent over and over again. 'I haven't seen you there lately.'

'I've been busy.'

'Oh.' Probably avoiding her at all costs. She decided to get out of there before he could officially turn her down. 'So I'll see you there. Around eight? Good. I have to run.' She forced her legs to move away from him, smiling brightly as she left. 'Catch you later.' With that, she quickly delivered her payment to Wesley who was suitably impressed with the number of frogs.

'You're really serious about this guy, aren't you?'

'Yes.' Annie shrugged. 'I'm in love with him.'

Wesley nodded. 'I hope it works out.'

Annie was surprised by his sincerity. 'Thanks. Well, I'd better go get some sleep.'

She left Wesley's office, which was smaller than hers, and almost ran the entire way home.

On Wednesday she felt renewed with energy and purpose. Tonight she would be with Hayden. First, though, she had to get through a day of clinics and meetings because she'd swapped shifts with Wesley.

In the hour she had between the end of her night-shift and the beginning of her day-shift, Annie raced home to shower and change. She dressed with care in one of her lightweight summer suits, turned her nose up at the curls she could do nothing to tame and brushed her teeth twice, to make sure they would be nice and bright when she smiled at him.

She practised those smiles in the mirror for a few seconds before closing her eyes and shaking her head. She opened them again and stared at her reflection.

'What are you doing?' she whispered. The answer was, she had no idea. She wanted to talk to Hayden, to try and show him that things would be different between the two of them than they had been between him and his ex-wife.

She knew this for a fact. She'd had countless relationships and each one had failed. Still, she'd been willing to go another round and this time she'd hit the jackpot. Even though she was sure he didn't want to hear what she had to say, she needed to say it—for her own piece of mind.

She glanced at her watch and realised with a start that if she didn't hustle, she was going to be late.

When she walked onto the ward just before the round began, she felt butterflies whizzing around her stomach. When Hayden raised his eyebrows momentarily, acknowledging her presence, the butterflies zoomed into overdrive and for a second Annie actually thought she was going to vomit.

The round proceeded without dramas. Mr Bouchard was out of CCU and would be in traction for the next few weeks. The physiotherapists were happy with his progress and everything looked rosy. Afterwards she headed to her office and caught up on some paperwork before going to Theatre to do the elective list.

Throughout the morning she slowly settled her stomach and ate lunch in the cafeteria with Natasha.

'You look stressed,' her friend commented.

'So much is riding on this evening.' She looked down at the salad roll she'd ordered and had taken three bites out of. 'I don't think I can finish this.' Annie pushed it away. 'What if it all backfires, Tash? What if what I have to say means nothing and he doesn't change his mind?' Tears started to well in her eyes.

'What have you got on this afternoon?'

'Clinic.'

'Well, at least you have something solid to concentrate on to get you through.' Natasha reached over and took her friend's hand in hers. 'Believe in yourself. Believe in yourself, Annie, and things will turn out right.'

Annie sighed and wiped away her tears.

Hayden was sitting at his desk, looking down at the paperwork in front of him, not registering a thing that was written there. She'd changed shifts with Wesley. She'd asked him out this evening. She looked incredibly beautiful today and he found her even harder to resist.

The knock at the door startled him and for a brief second he wished it was Annie, dreading it at the same time. 'Come,' he called, and relaxed visibly when Brenton walked into the room. 'Problem?'

'Just one of the interns wanting to switch an A and E placement with an orthopaedic placement. I needed to stretch my legs so I thought I'd bring it up instead of sticking it in the internal mail.' He handed Hayden the form.

Hayden scanned it. 'Looks fine.' He placed it in his in box. 'Anything else?'

'Yes. You may think I'm interfering, which is something I usually leave up to my wife.'

Hayden smiled. 'But…'

'But I just wanted you to know that Annie has applied for several jobs outside this hospital.'

Hayden nodded. 'That's natural. She finishes her training

in a few months so it's only right she looks for a new position. After all, she'll be a qualified consultant.'

'She's mentioned trying to get her six-month rotation here split into two lots of three, which means she'll be finishing at this hospital in about four weeks' time, at the end of March.'

Hayden absorbed the information, determined not to let his true emotions show.

'Just wanted to give you a "heads up".'

'Thanks.' He watched as Brenton headed for the door, knowing there was more to come. He was right. Brenton stopped, his hand on the door.

'Due to circumstances, completely different from yours, it took Natasha and I seven years before we could get to the point where we were happy. That's almost ten years ago now, and each day since then has proved to me it was worth the fight, worth the sacrifices and worth the pain, because now I have her love for ever.'

'Your point?'

'If things feel right with Annie, if you love her...' Brenton shook his head. 'Don't let true happiness escape you. Your life will never be the same again.'

Hayden nodded. 'Noted.'

Annie walked into the pool hall just before eight. Being a Wednesday night, it was typically quiet but Trevor welcomed her warmly.

'Back to shoot your sorrows away?'

'Better than drowning them.' She forced a smile and shrugged her shoulders. 'Table two free?'

'Kept it just for you.'

Annie glanced behind her at the door, willing Hayden to walk in. He'd paged her after clinic, saying he'd had a meeting rescheduled at the last minute and that he'd meet her at the pool hall when he was done. She wondered if it was just an excuse. Was he about to stand her up?

She headed over to the table and set everything up.

'Stop glaring at the door,' Trevor said as he brought over her usual lemonade. 'He'll get here when he gets here.'

'Is it that obvious?'

'That you're waiting for him, or that you're in love?'

Annie tried to laugh but it ended on a sigh. 'Both.'

'This is the real deal?'

'The real deal,' she repeated despondently, and slammed the tip of her cue into the white ball, scattering the rest of the balls around the table. Two found their homes in the pockets.

'Nice break. Want some company?'

'Thanks, but I don't want to drag you down into my misery.'

Trevor laughed. 'Surely it's not *that* bad.'

Annie sighed again. 'Ever been in love, Trev? *Really* in love?'

'Gee. I think I need to wipe the bar down again.' He moved in that direction and Annie smiled. 'At least I got you smiling.' He winked and turned away.

Annie bent over the table and concentrated on her shots. She potted another one. Geometry had always been one of her better subjects. She was beginning to think she'd completely flunked out in the 'affairs of the heart' class. Pity they hadn't offered *that* at university.

She slowly sank each ball in turn, playing mind games with herself. She wouldn't look over to the door until she'd potted another three balls.

Three balls down—she checked.

No Hayden.

She racked them up again and began the slow torture once more. She leaned over the table, determined that her eyes *wouldn't* fill with tears while she was trying to concentrate. Where was he? She'd been here almost an hour and deep down inside she was wondering just how long she was going to hang around. She knew the answer—until Trevor closed the place.

The door had opened a few times and each time she'd

looked over, her breath catching in her throat, only to hiss out slowly and dejectedly when it hadn't been Hayden. Angelo had stopped by to say hello and had asked after her friend. She hadn't been game enough to tell him she was supposed to meet Hayden—just in case he didn't show up.

'Focus,' she whispered to herself. She'd initially suggested the pool hall because the atmosphere relaxed her. Now, though, she realised it wouldn't have mattered where she'd suggested, she'd still be as nervous as she was now. She had a lot she wanted to say to him, but him showing up would be a huge step in the right direction.

Trevor brought her over another drink and the pitying look was almost too much to bear. Annie could feel anger starting to build. Who was Hayden's meeting with anyway, and at this time of night? Had it just been an excuse? No. She dismissed that thought. Hayden was man enough to tell her straight out if he wanted to cancel, and she couldn't really see him being the type to stand her up. He had principles, ethics and morals, and she loved him for that.

Still… She glanced over at the door, her jaw dropping open as she saw him walk in. Was she dreaming? Hallucinating? She didn't dare take her gaze off him in case he vanished into thin air. He didn't smile as he walked in her direction but instead he continued to a chair, dumped his briefcase on the ground and picked out a cue.

'I didn't think that meeting would ever end.' His voice was gruff and impatient as he chalked his cue. He looked at her and felt a blow to the solar plexus as he realised her eyes had filled with tears. 'Sorry I'm so late. I would have paged you but it was impossible and in the end I thought it better just to get the meeting over and done with and get here as soon as I could.'

Annie smiled…*really* smiled for the first time that day. 'That's OK.' She forgave him for being late. She forgave him for making her cry—in fact, she forgave him everything simply because he was there. She pulled a tissue from her pocket and dabbed at her eyes and sniffed. 'I'm just glad you came.'

He stayed on the other side of the table, needing distance in case he gave in to the urge to crush her to him. 'I didn't mean to…worry you.'

'You're here.' She busied herself with collecting the balls and settling the triangle around them. 'You break.'

'Sure.'

He broke and for the next few minutes Annie was happy simply to concentrate on the game. Hayden was here. He hadn't stood her up, and just being in his presence made her happy. What she wanted to say could wait until they'd both unwound.

Neither of them spoke much during the next two games, each winning one. As Hayden racked the balls up for another round, he looked at Annie.

'You wanted to talk?'

Annie's palms started to perspire. 'Yes.'

He nodded and, after removing the triangle, leaned over to break. The sounds of the balls clacking into each other was the only sound. Now what was she supposed to say? I think you've made a mistake? I think we should not only date but get married? I love you so much that if you don't my heart is going to break, and I don't think it will ever mend?

While she gathered her thoughts Hayden continued to pot the balls, not looking at her. 'Brenton mentioned you're thinking about doing two three-monthly stints to finish off your training.'

Annie closed her eyes. Typical of Monty. He probably thought he was helping, telling Hayden that piece of news. 'Yes. I was waiting to hear back from another hospital, you know, to see if it was actually possible before I told you.'

He bent over, targeting another ball, still not looking at her. 'Where?'

'Uh…Melbourne.'

'Got some friends there who can pull a few strings?'

'Yes.'

He didn't say anything else until he'd cleared the table. Then he stood, resting his cue on the floor. 'Why?'

'Why? How can you ask that?' Annie was astounded. 'Hayden, I love you and the fact that you don't return that love interferes with my professional life. I know it shouldn't and I've been working hard to separate the two, but the fact remains that we work together. You're my boss and you can't keep me working the evening on-call for ever.'

'So you're just going to leave.' He tossed his cue onto the table and stared at her.

'I think it's for the best.'

'You're a good doctor, Annie. The hospital needs you.'

'You'll be getting an equally competent replacement when I go.'

'And when will that be?'

'Well, if I can get everything organised, in about four weeks' time.'

'That's not long.'

'It's long enough.'

'What about your apartment?'

'I'll need something closer to the hospital.'

'And your friends? Are you going to uproot the Worthington family and take them to Melbourne, too?'

She frowned at him, slightly puzzled by his attitude. 'Anyone would think you care, Hayden.'

'I do care!' He slammed his hand down onto the table. Thankfully, the noise in the place had increased so no one noticed.

Annie's heart was beating wildly at his reaction. He cared...but how much? She closed her eyes momentarily, sending up a silent prayer. Hoping against hope. She opened them slowly, to watch him down his drink and rake a hand through his hair.

'Fill in the paperwork and give it to my secretary when you're done.' He stalked over to the chair and picked up his briefcase. He walked towards her and Annie felt as though she were slap-bang in the middle of her worst nightmare. He stopped and looked at her. 'If this is what you want.'

'It isn't.' Her tone was imploring, wanting him to know she was only doing this to keep herself from shrivelling up inside. 'I don't see I have much of a choice, Hayden. Working alongside you, living next door to you. You're driving me insane and the fact that you don't seem to want me—'

'I do.' His tone was as fierce as her own. He gripped her arm with his free hand. 'I do, Annie.'

Her heart lurched with renewed hope. It was there in his eyes. Yes, he wanted her but did he love her?

'I love you, Annie.' The words were said softly and his hand relaxed, rubbing up and down her arm. Her eyes glazed over with tears. There was her answer but the next question was—how much? 'Stay.' It was a whispered command and one she felt herself crumbling towards.

'And what?' she whispered back. 'Just hang around together? Move in together?' She shook her head. 'That's not my style, Hayden. I'm a traditional girl at heart and I want...I *need* the real deal. Marriage *and* children.'

He dropped his hand as though burnt, his eyes turning emotionless once more. 'Self-preservation. We each do what's necessary.' With that, he walked past her and headed towards the door.

Annie couldn't look. Couldn't watch him walk away.

Out of her life...for ever.

One week later, Annie had renegotiated her lease to expire at the end of March, even though it meant paying extra. She'd even stayed quite a few nights with the Worthingtons, unable to be so close to Hayden yet so far. Thankfully, neither Brenton nor Natasha had tried to change her mind. Katrina had even offered to speak to her stubborn brother on Annie's behalf, but Annie had made her new friend promise to keep her mouth shut.

Everything hurt, painfully so, but she kept telling herself it was for the best—self-preservation.

The paperwork to transfer the last three months of her training to Melbourne General was complete—except for Hayden's signature. Her replacement was all organised and she couldn't believe it had actually come to this. She dropped the forms off with his secretary at the end of her shift and fled before she burst into tears.

The hospital grapevine had noticed a huge difference in their new orthopaedic professor and his female registrar. Even Wesley was being nice to her in his own way. Amazingly enough, Annie didn't give a hoot about the gossip. She had better things to worry about, such as how to stop her heart from feeling like a dry piece of rock, heavy and burdensome.

On Saturday night, two days after she'd left the paperwork with his secretary, she ordered herself a pizza and sat in front of the television to devour it *and* a block of chocolate. Comfort food. At the moment it was her only consolation. Unfortunately, the movie was a love story and she wished she'd stopped by the video store to rent a comedy.

A knock at the door startled her, and as she sniffed and wiped tears from her eyes she walked over to open it.

'Hayden!' She stared, open-mouthed, unable to believe he was knocking on her door. The air seemed to rush from her lungs and her head started to feel light. When she started to sway, he leaned forward to support her.

'You all right?'

She took a wobbly step back from him, his touch scalding her. 'Fine.' She forced her instantly mushy heart to harden. 'What do you want? Cup of sugar?'

He smiled and that did it. She was lost. Her heart pounded its rhythm of love and her eyes glazed over with desire. Disgusted with herself and her body's traitorous reaction, she turned and shuffled her way back to the sofa.

'You look…comfortable.'

She glanced down at her old tracksuit, comfortable T-shirt and fluffy red slippers. She shrugged and turned the television off. 'Pizza?'

'No.' He closed her door behind him and walked over.

'What do you want?'

'To apologise.'

'For?'

He raked a hand through his hair. 'For being…an idiot.'

'No argument.'

He paced up and down her living room, looking so agitated that she couldn't help but take pity on him. 'Do you still love me?' She couldn't believe her voice cracked and quickly cleared her throat.

He stopped and crouched down near the sofa. 'Yes.'

Annie closed her eyes and sighed thankfully. Her eyes opened again when he lifted her legs and sat on the sofa beside her, placing her legs over his. 'I love you,' he said sincerely, and cupped her face in his hands. 'The past week and a half has been the most miserable of my life.'

'I know. I've lived it, too.'

He brushed his thumb over her mouth and looked pleadingly into her eyes. 'I need to kiss you, Annie. It's eating me alive. I can't think, I can't work, I can't sleep. I need to kiss you,' he whispered, and before she could say anything, his mouth was on hers.

Where she thought it might be hard and furious, she was wrong. He was tender, gentle and, above all, passionate. It was a kiss of promise. A kiss of hope. And her own emotions started soaring out of control.

Her heart filled with love and she returned his kiss, emotion for emotion, showing him how completely wonderful it was to have his mouth against hers once more.

He pulled back, gasping for air. 'The thought of never being able to kiss you again ate away at my heart. Regardless of what I've said in the past, regardless of what I've done to hurt you, the thought of never being able to hold you, to kiss you, to be with you…makes me feel like an empty shell.' His hands caressed her face again, his thumb rubbing sensually over her swollen lips as he spoke.

Impatiently, he turned her around and dragged her onto his lap, his arms holding her firmly to him as though he was never going to let her go. 'I love you, Annie.'

'So you've said.' She needed to let him know that there *had* to be more. He'd told her he loved her before and had still broken her heart.

'You were right when you accused me of merely existing instead of living. I am…was. That's what I'm here to change.'

'Hayden, I—'

'No. You were right, Annie. After Liana's death, I locked everything up. My heart, my emotions, my passion. Lonnie had destroyed her fair share but Liana's death…it tipped me over the edge.'

Annie watched him closely, seeing and feeling his pain as he spoke. She gently pushed his hair back from his face, loving the feel of it beneath her fingers.

'I can't do this any more.' Hayden's voice broke and she gathered him closer, burying her head in his neck. She kissed him, breathed him in and felt herself getting stronger.

'You don't have to,' she said a moment later, pulling back to look down into his eyes. 'Whatever you need to face, whatever you need to sort out, let's do it together. Don't shut me out any more, Hayden.'

'I won't. I can't. I need you, Annie.' He pressed his lips to hers. 'I don't deserve you.'

'Oh, yes, you do,' she answered quickly. 'You're a good man, Hayden, and you deserve the best, if I do say so myself.'

He smiled at her, relaxing with her firmly in his embrace. 'And you are, Annie. You are the best…for me.' He breathed in and slowly exhaled, all the while mesmerised by her. 'You are one special lady.' He kissed her again. 'I didn't want to hurt you, never intentionally, but in the end I did and was surprised when it hurt me just as much. You can't go. You can't leave me. I tore up the paperwork.'

'You didn't!'

'I did. I was furious you'd gone through with it. Furious that you were daring to survive without me. I knew I'd pushed you to do it and it was then I knew it was wrong. Everything I'd thought, fought against for years was wrong. *You* were the only *right* thing in my world and I'd done an excellent job of pushing you away.'

She tightened her hold on him. 'I'm still here, aren't I?'

'Where you belong.'

'Yes.' Annie took a deep breath and asked, 'How about if I stay right here in your arms for…hmm…I don't know, about the next fifty or sixty years?'

'At our age?' He chuckled. 'We'd be one hundred after sixty years of marriage.'

'I think we can handle it.' It was then she realised he'd said the 'M' word. She sat up straighter. 'Did you just say…?'

'Marriage? Yes, I did.' Hayden took her hands in his. 'I didn't want to get married again or have children because I couldn't bear to fail again. I'd failed as a husband and as a father already, and in taking a chance with you I would be risking failure once more.'

'You didn't fail as a father,' Annie whispered. 'I'm positive Liana not only knew she was loved but felt it. It wasn't your fault she died.'

'She was a good baby, quiet and happy, and she looked so peaceful when I checked on her only a few hours before.'

Annie looked at the man before her, not at all surprised to see tears in his eyes. 'Then she left you, carried away on the wings of angels to a far, far better place. Hayden, you were a good father and I'm not just saying that because I want to have children with you. I've seen the way you are with your nieces and nephews. They adore you. I've seen how you care for your patients, how you cared for me when I was sick.'

'I don't know if I can bear to have another child.' Annie kissed him, putting all the reassurance she could into it. 'I want to and I want you to be the mother, but I still don't know.'

'Regardless of what may happen in our future, we'll be handling it *together*. You're my soul mate, Hayden. I need to be with you as much as I need to breathe, and I'm never going to leave.' She kissed him again. 'Trust me. Trust me, Hayden.'

'I do.' He kissed her back then gazed into her eyes. 'You humble me, Annie, and you make me want to be a better person. Not only when I'm with you but when I'm at work, with my family—all the time. I have a huge debt to repay.' He nodded with determination. 'And I'm going to start right now.'

He cradled her in his arms and stood before gently lowering her to her feet. 'Come with me.'

'What?' Annie was a little confused but followed him nevertheless. 'Hayden?'

He picked up her keys and walked to the front door. He opened it and, holding her hand firmly, took her out into the corridor. He dug out his own keys from his pocket and unlocked his apartment door.

'What's going on?'

'Close your eyes.' She frowned at him and he moved closer, putting his arm securely around her shoulders. 'You'll be fine. Trust me, Annie.' He kissed the tip of her nose. 'And close your eyes.'

'OK.' She leaned into him before lowering her eyelids, her ears listening for any clue to what was going on. The last time he'd done this, she'd received a wonderful dress. It had been an overwhelming surprise and now…she had that same feeling churning around with the nervous butterflies in her stomach.

He urged her forward, over the threshold, before closing the door behind them.

'Hayden?'

'A little bit further.' She heard him flick the light switch. 'Open your eyes.'

Annie gasped in wonderment, her jaw hanging open. His apartment had changed somewhat since she'd last been over. Around the floor, on his desk, on the comfortable chairs were chocolate frogs!

She laughed in amazement, her hands covering her mouth. 'I can't believe this.' There were also six or seven large florist's boxes of gerberas around the room, brightening it up and contrasting with the shiny chocolate frog wrappers.

She turned to look at him. 'Oh, Hayden.' She laughed again. 'You really *are* a romantic at heart.'

He bent and kissed her. 'Only with you.'

Annie leaned into him, utterly content. 'I can't eat all of them by myself. You are going to have to help me.'

'This is just the beginning, Annie.'

'There are more chocky frogs?'

'No.' He led her over to one of his luxurious chairs. 'Have a seat.'

Annie lifted the frogs off the chair before she sat. 'More surprises?'

'Yes.' He walked carefully through the scattered frogs to his desk, opened a drawer and pulled out a flat, rectangular box. 'Here.'

'Are you sure I don't need to close my eyes for his one?'

Hayden chuckled at her teasing. 'No. I want them wide open.'

Annie accepted the box and carefully lifted the lid. 'Hayden…' She could feel her lower lip begin to tremble as she stared at the present. 'It's perfect.' She trailed her finger around the edge of the gold heart-shaped photo frame which held a picture of herself and Hayden taken at Rowena's wedding.

'Turn it over.'

'What? The frame?'

'Yes.'

Annie took it out of the box and there, tied to the black stand, was a diamond ring. She glanced up at him, totally flabbergasted.

He moved, lowering himself to one bended knee, and Annie couldn't resist smiling. She was totally surprised by his romantic streak but loved it all the same.

'I love you, Annie. Marry me. Build a home with me. Build a life with me.'

She touched the ring, biting her lower lip to stop the quivering. Taking a deep breath, she angled her head and eyed him thoughtfully, pretending to consider his request. 'Will your mother make her mouthwatering pancakes?'

Hayden smiled. 'I can guarantee it.'

'And we can do the whole prewedding family breakfast, even if it's considered bad luck for the bride and groom to see each other before the wedding?'

'I have an idea.' He pulled her up out of the chair, settled himself in her place and then tugged her back down onto his lap. 'Why don't we make the wedding a breakfast wedding?'

'Wouldn't that be too much work for your mother?'

Hayden laughed. 'No. She thrives on that kind of thing and I wouldn't be surprised if she's already started planning it.'

Hayden unhooked the ring from the frame and took Annie's left hand in his. 'This is for life, Annie.' He gently pushed the ring onto the third finger. 'For life and for ever.'

With that, he gathered her close and kissed her like there was no tomorrow. Annie melted into his embrace, her mouth moving over his with a renewal of her love. Their passions met and united, taking them both to dizzying heights neither had dreamed of.

Hayden broke his mouth from hers and buried his head

in her neck. 'You will definitely have to marry me soon.'
He nipped her ear lobe.

'Why?' She pulled back to look at him.

'Well, you can't expect to kiss me like that just for *fun*
and get away with it!' His blue eyes twinkled with love
and Annie's breath caught in her throat.

She hugged him tight and looked around the room. It
was then she froze, her eyes growing as wide as saucers.
'Eww.'

'What?'

'Spider!'

'Where?' He started chuckling.

She pointed, looking the other way.

'It's only a small one.' He looked at the eight-legged
creature crawling around the ceiling.

'Eww.'

He laughed again, lifted her from his lap, placed her back
in the chair and went to the kitchen. 'Huntsmen aren't all
that bad,' he said as he came back with a glass.

'Yeah? How so?'

'They travel in twos, remember. They find their mate and
stay together for life. Just like the two of us. Together for
life.'

'Well, could they do it somewhere else?' Annie hunched
herself up on the chair, closing her eyes, glad Hayden was
around to take care of it. 'Make sure you find the other
one, too.'

She stayed where she was until he returned from taking
the spiders outside. Hayden laughed as he gathered her
close.

'All taken care of.'

She kissed him. 'My knight in shining armour.'

'You know, you still haven't answered my question.'

'What question?'

'Whether or not you'll marry me!'

'Oh. Haven't I? How remiss of me.'

'Well?'

'OK. I *will* marry you but just don't ever group the two of us with those eight-legged things again! Eww.'

Hayden laughed. 'Being married to you, Annie, is going to be…'

'Stressful?'

He shook his head.

'Challenging?'

'That wasn't what I was going to say.'

'Well?'

'Being married to you is going to be…*perfect*.'

EPILOGUE

'EXCUSE me.' Brenton tapped the side of his champagne glass. 'Quiet, please.'

Everyone at the long table in Eloise's and Mike's back garden stopped their conversations to listen. Kelly and Matt sat with their children, along with Natasha and the rest of the Worthington clan.

Hayden's sisters and their families were smiling happily at their new sister-in-law. Eloise and Mike had welcomed her warmly the instant they'd learned of her engagement to their son. Annie's 'family' was almost complete.

All that was missing were children of her own, but who knew what would happen during their planned honeymoon at the Great Barrier Reef?

They'd decided to wait until Annie had finished her orthopaedic rotation and qualified before getting married. Both she and Hayden had honoured her transfer to Melbourne General for three months, and although the commute had been stressful at times, it was now over.

'As the person who has known the bride the longest, it's only fair that I get to toast her first,' Brenton said. 'To the woman who saved my reputation in high school by putting herself…and her nose…on the line.'

They all laughed and Annie shook her finger at him.

'She is an amazing woman and I'm honoured to call her one of my dearest friends for over twenty years. Thank you for your friendship. It's a precious gift and one I, my wife and our children will always treasure.' He inclined his glass towards Hayden. 'And to the groom—thank goodness you came to your senses!'

Hayden laughed as everyone else chorused their approval.

Annie didn't even try to stop the tears that twinkled on the edges of her lashes, knowing Hayden would always be there to tenderly wipe them away.

Her husband rose to his feet, his glass also raised. 'Thank you, Brenton. As the husband of the bride, I would also like to propose a toast to my wife.' He gazed down at her, his eyes filled with the unconditional love that would always make her heart race.

'Annie, you gave me a second chance at happiness, at love and, more importantly, at life. You are truly a special person and I'm honoured that you're my wife.' He glanced around the table at their *family*. 'I'm sure everyone here agrees just how special you are because in some unique way you've touched us all. Each and every one of us at some point has been privileged by your inner strength, your spirit and your natural ability to give so selflessly.

'I love you, Annie, and I always will.' Hayden bent his head and claimed her lips possessively, tenderly wiping away her tears of sheer joy.

Everyone stood and raised their glasses to the blushing bride. Annie's heart filled up with love and bubbled over. She had never, in her wildest dreams, thought she could be so happy—yet she was.

'To the bride and groom.' They all chorused.

'To Annie,' Hayden said softly beside her. 'My love. My soul mate. My wife.'

LIVE THE EMOTION

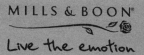

MILLS & BOON®

Live the emotion

Medical Romance™

OUTBACK ENCOUNTER *by Meredith Webber*

As a research scientist, Dr Caitlin O'Shea's usual problem is not being taken seriously – her stunning blonde looks get in the way! But she's not expecting her work in tiny Outback town Turalla to have so many other challenges – like Connor Clarke, the town's overworked doctor…

THE NURSE'S RESCUE *by Alison Roberts*

Paramedic Joe Barrington was determined not to give in to his attraction for nurse Jessica McPhail – he just couldn't get involved with a mother, and Jessica had to put her child Ricky first. But when Joe risked his life to rescue Ricky, he and Jessica realised that the bond between them was growing stronger by the day.

A VERY SINGLE MIDWIFE *by Fiona McArthur*

Beautiful midwife Bella Wilson has recently regained her independence – and she doesn't want obstetrician Scott Rainford confusing things. Twelve years ago their relationship ended painfully, and she won't let him hurt her all over again. But now, working side by side, they find their feelings for each other are as strong as ever…

On sale 6th February 2004

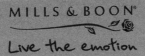

4 FREE

books and a surprise gift!

We would like to take this opportunity to thank you for reading this Mills & Boon® book by offering you the chance to take FOUR more specially selected titles from the Medical Romance™ series absolutely FREE! We're also making this offer to introduce you to the benefits of the Reader Service™—

- ★ FREE home delivery
- ★ FREE gifts and competitions
- ★ FREE monthly Newsletter
- ★ Exclusive Reader Service offers
- ★ Books available before they're in the shops

Accepting these FREE books and gift places you under no obligation to buy, you may cancel at any time, even after receiving your free shipment. Simply complete your details below and return the entire page to the address below. *You don't even need a stamp!*

YES! Please send me 4 free Medical Romance books and a surprise gift. I understand that unless you hear from me, I will receive 6 superb new titles every month for just £2.60 each, postage and packing free. I am under no obligation to purchase any books and may cancel my subscription at any time. The free books and gift will be mine to keep in any case.

M4ZED

Ms/Mrs/Miss/Mr ....Initials.....................................
BLOCK CAPITALS PLEASE

Surname ....

Address ....

....

....Postcode.................................

Send this whole page to:
UK: FREEPOST CN81, Croydon, CR9 3WZ
EIRE: PO Box 4546, Kilcock, County Kildare (stamp required)